ROOM FOR A STRANGER

ANN TURNBULL

WALKER BOOKS
AND SUBSIDIARIES
LONDON • BOSTON • SYDNEY

First published 1996 by Walker Books Ltd
87 Vauxhall Walk, London SE11 5HJ

2 4 6 8 10 9 7 5 3 1

This book has been typeset in Sabon.

Printed in England

British Library Cataloguing in Publication Data
A catalogue record for this book is available from the British Library.

ISBN 0-7445-4128-X

ROOM FOR A STRANGER

Other books by the same author

No Friend of Mine

Pigeon Summer

Summer of the Cats

Trouble with Bats

To
Gina Pollinger

CHAPTER ONE

Doreen turned the corner into Lion Street and saw a car parked outside her home.

The doctor! she thought. And she felt alarmed.

But it wasn't the doctor's car; she realized that almost at once. Then whose could it be? No one else she knew had a car.

She ran towards the house, but before she reached it the visitor came out: a woman, small, grey-haired; a stranger. She got into the car and drove away towards Station Road.

Rosie Lloyd next door stood in her front yard, staring, a skipping rope loose in her hands. She wiped her nose on her sleeve as Doreen approached, and said, "A lady came to see your mum."

"Who was she?"

"Don't know. Can I come round?"

"No." Doreen darted down the covered

passageway between the two houses and in through the back door. "Mum! Mum, who was that?"

Her mother came out of the front room, carrying a tray with tea things on it. Someone important, then, Doreen thought.

Mum put the tray on the draining board. "That was Miss Wingfield, the Billeting Officer."

"Billeting Officer?"

"You know, for the evacuees. She finds billets for them – places to stay."

"You mean...?"

"We're going to have an evacuee."

Doreen stared at her. "But – I don't want one!" She hadn't realized until now how strongly she felt this. "Why do we have to have one?"

"Oh, Doreen!" Mum rounded on her. "You went on and on about *wanting* an evacuee when the war started."

That had been in 1939 – two years ago – when the evacuees first came; when all her friends had been getting them and Doreen had felt left out.

"I've gone off them," she said. "They have nits."

"You've had nits."

"They pinch things. And swear. And they pong."

She became aware of Rosie Lloyd, with her

skipping rope twined round her, standing outside the open back door.

"Go home, Rosie," she said. "I'm not playing."

Rosie drifted a few yards away and began to skip half-heartedly.

"Most of them aren't like that," said Mum. "There's Maura O'Brien; she's nice. And little Shirley. And Mrs Mullen's boys."

She turned away to wash the tea cups.

"I felt," she explained, "that I ought to say yes. We couldn't have anyone before, with your dad being so ill, but now that he's ... gone, and we've got the space..."

Her voice was tight, and Doreen thought of Dad and felt a lump in her own throat.

Mum went on. "Miss Wingfield's got some kiddies need moving quickly – foster mother taken ill. So I said we'd help." She turned back to Doreen. "It'll be a girl –"

"What girl? What's her name? How old is she?"

"I don't know yet; Miss Wingfield hasn't sorted out who's going where. But I did say to her, 'It'll have to be a girl; she'll be sharing a bedroom with Doreen' – "

"Sharing my room!"

It was only in the last year or so that Doreen had had the bedroom to herself. Before that she'd been squashed up at one end in a camp bed, with a screen separating her from her two grown-up sisters. But Phyl had got married, and then Mary had joined the WAAF, and now she only had to share when Mary came home on leave.

"What about Mary?" she demanded, producing her sister like an ace from a hand of cards.

But Mum said, "Mary's no problem. When she's home she can bunk in with me."

Doreen conceded defeat. "So when's she coming – this girl?"

"Friday night."

Friday. And this was Monday evening.

"If you want to do something useful," said Mum, "you could turn out the drawers in your dressing-table. Make a bit of space."

Doreen scuffed at the fender with her shoe. Why should she? None of this was her idea.

"Unless you want me to do it," said Mum.

"No!"

Doreen ran upstairs.

Two rooms opened on either side of the tiny landing: Mum's and hers.

Why should *she* have to share? Why not Mum? Why not Lennie?

She shouted down the stairs, "Why don't you get a boy to share with Lennie?"

She knew why as soon as she said it: Lennie slept in the front room, on a camp bed that had to be packed up and put away every morning. There was no space for anyone else in there.

It's all right for Lennie, she thought.

She pushed open the door of her room.

There were two beds, two chairs and a dressing-table; a rail across one corner with boxes underneath formed a makeshift wardrobe. Most of the clothes in it were Mary's civvies. All Doreen possessed was a change of clothes and what Mum called her Sunday dress.

Which bed would Mum give to the girl? she wondered. Doreen slept in the one nearest the window. The other had a spring that caught you under the ribs when you lay on your right side. She decided that if Mum thought the girl should have the window bed she'd get Lennie to help her change the mattresses round.

Tidy up; make space, Mum had said. Well, she could start with Mary's junk. She opened the dressing-table drawers and took out some stockings with holes in the toes, a handbag, a hairbrush, a dingy bra. She piled them on the floor.

On top of the dressing-table were scraps of paper on which Doreen had begun stories or designed film posters. She picked up a crayoned picture of palm trees and pyramids surrounding the words

DESERT SONG
starring DOREEN DYER

Doreen Dyer. You couldn't be a film star

with a name like that. She wished she had a romantic name: Amanda Daly; or Ann Hamilton.

She wondered what the evacuee's name was. She hoped it wasn't Mavis. The Ansons had a Mavis and she was awful. Isla would be better; she'd read that in a book. Surely no one called Isla would have nits or wet the bed.

She gathered up all her papers and hid them away in the top right-hand drawer. She didn't want the girl getting hold of them and making fun of her ideas. She dusted the dressing-table with an old vest of Mary's and moved her own hairbrush and comb to the right-hand side.

Mum came upstairs. "How are you doing? I'll give you a hand."

Doreen realized that Mum was trying to smooth things over, but she didn't want to be smoothed – not yet.

"I've finished," she said, putting on an injured voice. "She's got both those drawers and half the top and I suppose she'll have loads of clothes to put in the wardrobe."

"I doubt it," said Mum. "But I'll take Mary's clothes and put them in mine. You know, Doreen, I'm not doing this because I *want* another child in the house. I just felt we should help. It'll need an effort from all of us."

But especially me, thought Doreen.

She followed Mum into the other bedroom and watched her hanging up Mary's clothes.

Dad's shirts and trousers still hung there. Mum pushed them along the rail. Her hand lingered on the last one. "I suppose I ought to give these away."

Doreen heard the click of the back gate.

"Here's Lennie!" She ran downstairs to tell him.

Lennie was wheeling his bicycle into the shed. He was unmoved by Doreen's news.

"I've got to call the birds in," he said, moving past her towards the pigeon loft.

Doreen followed him. "Lennie, you're just *pretending* not to be interested."

"It won't make any difference to me."

No, it won't, Doreen thought. I'll be the one who has some kid hanging around all the time. But she'd wanted support and sympathy from Lennie; he never had time for her these days.

When Mum went off to work on Tuesday morning she left Doreen a shopping list. Doreen had got used to doing the shopping since the summer holidays had started. She enjoyed it.

She picked up the housekeeping purse and the ration book and went out early. She still felt apprehensive about the evacuee coming but she liked the idea of telling everyone.

She bought Spam, margarine, potatoes, dried eggs. In the butcher's shop, Mr Lee winked at her and brought out from under the counter a small pack of kidneys. That would please Mum.

She said, "We're getting an evacuee. Is Barbara there? I want to tell her."

"She's round the back, helping her mum. Go on through."

Doreen went into the back room. All the chopping up was done here, and it smelt of raw meat. Barbara and her mother were scrubbing the tabletops. Barbara wore an overall and her plaits were wound round her head like a factory girl's. She smiled when she saw Doreen.

Doreen told them her news. Mrs Lee said, "That'll be nice, Doreen. Someone for you to play with."

But Barbara looked downcast. "She'll go round with us, then," she said.

Doreen realized that Barbara was jealous. She was surprised, and pleased. "She's going to share my room," she told her.

Barbara didn't have an evacuee. There was a spare room, but it belonged to her brother, who had been killed at Dunkirk. It was rumoured among the Culverton children that nothing in the room had been moved since. Being bereaved gave Barbara status. Doreen hoped that having an evacuee might help her catch up.

At five-fifteen on Friday night Doreen was

mashing a small piece of corned beef into a lot of leftover cabbage and potato. There was more potato to go with it, and prunes for afters.

Lennie had just come home from work, hollow-eyed with exhaustion, and dropped into the armchair that used to be Dad's. Doreen made him a mug of tea; he took it in a hand ingrained with coal dust. "When's this girl coming, then?"

"After tea. Lennie, I feel all fluttery inside."

"Daft," said Lennie, but not unkindly.

"Well, I do. I'm sort of anxious but excited as well."

She turned the heat down under the potatoes and put some lard to melt in the frying pan. Mum had asked her to start cooking so that they'd be cleared away and tidy when Miss Wingfield arrived with the evacuee.

At a quarter to six Lennie said, "You'd better make a fresh pot of tea. Mum'll be here in a minute."

The hash was sticking to the pan; Doreen scraped at a burnt patch.

"Kettle's there, if you want to fill it," she said.

Lennie didn't move. He was stretched out with his feet on the fender, reading *The Dandy*. "I'm a working man now," he said.

"You're a lazy bugger," said Doreen, and at that moment Mum walked in.

Doreen felt herself going hot, but Mum was in a good mood and just said, "Language, Doreen!" and hung up her coat.

Doreen filled the kettle. "Well, he is," she said. "Mum, he won't even move his legs so I can reach things off the mantelpiece."

Lennie immediately moved them and went to sit at the table.

"Where's my tea?" he demanded, grinning.

"He's only teasing," said Mum. "If you didn't rise to it, he wouldn't do it."

Doreen knew it was true. But she glowered at Lennie as they ate.

"Doreen's in a tizzy about this evacuee," said Lennie.

"I'm not!" She counted her prune stones, hoping for a sailor: "Tinker, tailor, soldier, sailor, rich man ... poor man. I'm going to marry a poor man."

"That's a fair bet," said Mum. "Now listen, you two: when this girl comes, don't stare or ask too many questions. She'll probably be shy at first."

They cleared the table, and Lennie went back to *The Dandy*. Mum switched on the wireless and found the Light Programme, and she and Doreen sang along together as they washed up.

"You're a good little singer," said Mum. "Pity you can't come with me to choir practice."

Most Friday nights Mum went to the church hall to sing with the choir; she'd joined it after Dad died.

"Are you going tonight?" Doreen asked.

"Oh, no. Not with the— "

There was a knock at the door.

Mum struggled with her apron strings. "They're in a knot! Help me, Doreen."

Doreen freed her just as Lennie opened the door to Miss Wingfield.

"Hallo, everyone," said Miss Wingfield.

She ushered a girl into the room.

"This is Rhoda Kelly."

CHAPTER TWO

Rhoda Kelly was taller than Doreen, older-looking. She had red-gold hair, thick, curly and shoulder-length, and her face, which looked small under all the hair, was covered in freckles. Her eyes were pale blue. They flicked around as she entered the room, taking in everything, and finally coming to rest on Doreen. The two girls looked each other over in silence. Doreen felt intimidated. She wished Rhoda had been younger than her; just a bit younger: ten, perhaps.

Mum seemed nervous, too. She said, "Hallo, Rhoda. Come in, love. Let me take your coat. This is Lennie and this is Doreen. I'll put the kettle on. You'll stay for a cup of tea, Miss Wingfield?"

Miss Wingfield sat down at the kitchen table, forestalling any attempt on Mum's part to move them all into the front room. Doreen was relieved. It was cold in there, and there was nowhere to put your cup.

"Do you like tea, Rhoda?"

"Yes, please, Mrs Dyer."

Rhoda's voice was clear and confident.

"How big is this house?" she asked. She had a Liverpool accent.

"Two up, two down," said Mum. "You'll be sharing a room with Doreen."

"I've been staying in a big house in the country," said Rhoda. "Greenacres Farm. There were eight of us there."

"And you went to St Joseph's, didn't you?" prompted Miss Wingfield. "Rhoda's a Catholic," she explained. "We like to place them with Catholic families if we can, but it hasn't been possible every time. She'll go to St Joseph's – the Catholic school in Wraybury. She's brought her clothes in that bag, and if you need anything else we may be able to help. We can get you blankets..."

Rhoda caught Doreen's eye. "Can I see the house?"

They got up. Doreen glanced at Lennie, wanting him to come too, but he ignored her. It wasn't fair, Doreen thought, the way everyone saw Rhoda as her responsibility.

She opened the door of the front room, intending to give Rhoda a quick glimpse, but Rhoda walked in and started looking around, touching things. She picked up Nan Dyer's vase – the one she'd had as a wedding present. "This is nice." She stroked the worn plush of the armchair, skimmed a hand along the small shelf of books without reading the titles, and picked up a photograph from the sideboard. "Who's this, in uniform?"

"My sister Mary."

Doreen felt invaded. Who did she think she was, this Rhoda, poking her nose into everything?

"And that one – with the baby?"

"Phyl."

Rhoda discovered the oval mirror and studied her reflection in it, pushing back her hair.

Doreen said, "Do you want to see my room?"

They went back into the kitchen.

"Take your bag, Rhoda, if you're going up," said Mum.

Rhoda took the brown paper carrier bag and Doreen led the way up the steep twisting stairs. The door on the right was ajar. "That's Mum's room," she said, and to her alarm Rhoda walked in.

Doreen hovered by the door. "We don't usually come in this room unless Mum says."

But Rhoda took no notice. She flicked through the clothes on the rail and picked up Mum's brooch with the china roses and turned it in her hand. Doreen hoped Mum couldn't hear them moving around overhead.

"Where's your dad?" Rhoda asked.

"He's dead."

She didn't want to talk about Dad – not to Rhoda. But Rhoda's eyes had quickened with interest. "What did he die of?"

"The dust."

"The dust?"

"Down the mine. It gets on your lungs."

"Do you miss him?"

Doreen didn't answer.

"He's gone to Heaven," said Rhoda. "He's in a better place."

The Minister had said something of the sort at the funeral, Doreen remembered, but it wasn't the sort of thing they said at home; it made her feel uncomfortable.

Rhoda had found a photograph. "Is this their wedding day? Your mam was pretty."

Doreen became desperate to get Rhoda away. She knew Mum must be able to hear their voices. "Come and see my room."

She opened the door.

"Oh! You've got a triple mirror!" Rhoda exclaimed.

Doreen felt proud. "My sisters bought it between them. Second-hand."

Rhoda turned her attention to the beds.

"Which bed will I have? I like the pink patchwork."

"That one's mine," said Doreen.

"Is that your night-light?"

Doreen's night-light – a candle in a tin – was on the chair beside her bed. For the first time in her life she felt embarrassed by it – it seemed babyish; but then she had always been the baby of the family. "Will you mind it being on?"

"Are you afraid of the dark, then?"

"I just like it on," said Doreen. She didn't want to talk about her fears. "I've emptied those two drawers. And you can hang things on the rail."

Rhoda began to take out clothes: a faded summer frock, a blue cardigan, a pair of pink knickers embroidered with rosebuds. Doreen stared at the knickers.

"How old is your brother?" asked Rhoda.

"Fifteen."

"My boyfriend's twenty-two."

Doreen was astonished, both at his age and at the thought that Rhoda might be old enough to have a boyfriend at all. "That's old," she said. "How old are you?"

"Thirteen. My birthday's in February. I'm an Aquarius."

Doreen wanted to know more about the boyfriend, but she couldn't think what questions to ask.

"I'll be twelve in November," she said.

"What day?"

"The tenth."

"You're Scorpio, then."

Doreen had scarcely heard of the star signs, but she knew there was a horoscope page in Mum's magazine. She'd look up Scorpio, she decided.

Rhoda continued. "Sister Ursula says astrology is wickedness and leads to eternal damnation, but me mam always reads our horoscopes."

She took out a Bible and a rosary and put them on the chair beside her bed. On the dressing-table she placed a picture of the Virgin Mary with baby Jesus. The picture had bits of gold in it that glinted as it caught the light: gold haloes and sun's rays and an angel with gold tips to its wings.

They heard footsteps on the stairs, and Mum came in.

"Miss Wingfield's gone now. Is everything all right?"

"Yes," said Rhoda. "I like it here."

"There's a screen," said Mum, "if you prefer..."

"A screen?"

Mum pulled it out from behind the dressing-table. The screen was old, battered, covered in dark brown peeling paper. Over the years the children had pasted pictures on it: film stars, fashions, Christmas cards with robins and holly, and paper motifs from crackers.

Doreen loved its shabby familiarity. And she wanted it up; she wanted to make a space of her own where Rhoda couldn't come. But already Mum was pushing it back, saying, "You won't need it, will you? You'll want to talk." And Rhoda agreed.

"I'll leave you to it, then," said Mum. She went out.

Doreen followed, closing the door behind her. "Mum..."

Mum stopped on the stairs. "Don't whisper. It's rude."

"But I don't like her."

"That's silly. She seems quite all right. Nice and polite. Clean."

"She's..." Doreen struggled to express what she felt. She thought of the boyfriend. "She's older than me."

"I thought you'd like that. You're used to having older sisters."

But Rhoda wasn't a bit like her sisters, Doreen thought. They were grown-up; they babied her, gave way to her. Doreen could control her sisters.

"Go and make friends," said Mum. "You'll soon get on."

She turned away.

Reluctantly Doreen went back into the room.

Rhoda had finished unpacking. She had no coat, just a couple of summer frocks and a cardigan. But there was a dressing-gown: long, silky and patterned with roses. And her shoes were black patent with a narrow strap over the instep. Doreen always wore plimsolls. She made up her mind to try on those shoes when Rhoda wasn't around.

She noticed the other things Rhoda had put on her side of the dressing-table: a pot of face cream, a brush and comb, and a black and white photograph in a frame. The photograph showed a woman's face glancing back over one shoulder and smiling with glossy lips. She had light hair that billowed in curls.

"Who's that?"

"My mother."

"Your *mother*?" Doreen had assumed it was a film star.

Rhoda handed her the photograph. Doreen could see that she was proud of it. There was writing across one corner. Doreen read it aloud: "'Anne-Marie'. Is that her name? It's lovely."

"It's her stage name: not 'Anne-Marie Kelly' – just 'Anne-Marie'. Her real name's Mary Ann; she hates it."

"Is she a film star?"

"She's a singer and dancer. And she does some acting. She's quite well-known. I'm going to be a singer, too."

"So am I," said Doreen. "Or I might be an actress." An exciting possibility occurred to her: "Will your mother come and see you?"

"Oh, she's sure to. But she's doing the

summer season at the Hippodrome, so she won't have a lot of time."

"What's your house like in Liverpool?" Doreen asked. She imagined a grand place, like the mine owners' houses at Woodend.

But Rhoda said, "Oh – nothing. Just a room. Mam puts her things around: photos, and posters, and mirrors. But we're always moving."

Doreen was envious. "I've lived here all my life."

Rhoda looked out of the window. "Is that a mine?"

"Yes. That's Springhill pit head. Mum and Lennie both work there."

"Your mam too?"

Rhoda sounded astonished, and Doreen was glad to have the advantage for once. "Not digging coal," she said scornfully. "Mum works on the screens – sorting."

Rhoda changed the subject. "Have you got any shops? Big shops? Or arcades? Or cinemas?"

"There's a cinema," said Doreen. "We could go to Saturday morning pictures if you like. It gets crowded, though. All the vaccies – " She stopped, embarrassed. "Lots of little kids. They're fidgety, like."

"Our cinema was bombed," said Rhoda. "The seats gone, the walls, everything. There's just the arch and the stage left."

Doreen wished there had been a bomb on Culverton – just one, a small one. She sought for something that would equal a bomb site. "We could go to Old Works tomorrow," she said. "It's all ruins there, old buildings, a tunnel."

"A tunnel!"

"It's dangerous," said Doreen. "Don't tell Mum. She doesn't like me playing there."

CHAPTER THREE

"Doreen?" came Rhoda's voice. "Are you awake?"

"Yes."

"There's something hard in this bed."

"It's a spring."

"Gets you between the ribs," said Rhoda.

Doreen felt a mean satisfaction. At least she'd kept the best bed.

It was morning. She'd been lying awake for some time, listening to Rhoda's breathing. Rhoda sounded different to Mary, or Phyl, or Lennie. They all had their own, familiar sounds. But then Rhoda *was* different. She did strange things. Last night, wrapped in the silky dressing-gown, she had washed out her knickers and socks in the kitchen sink and hung them over the fireguard to dry. Then she had dabbed her face with cold cream, coiled her hair into pin curls secured with hair grips, and knelt at the side of her bed and murmured prayers.

Doreen had felt that she would like to say prayers, too, but she didn't know any words; and her hair was too short for pin curls.

Rhoda got out of bed.

She was wearing a white cotton nightdress with ribbon straps over the shoulders. Doreen thought it romantic; her own nightdress was flowered winceyette, grey with age.

Rhoda noticed her looking and said, "Do you like my nightie? I made it out of an old sheet. Dead easy. Bernadette showed me – me mam's dressmaker."

Doreen climbed on a chair and undid the pegs of the blackout screen and lifted it down. She pulled the curtains and pushed the window wider open, letting in mild summer air.

Outside, the day looked fine already, with blue sky and little high, white puffs of cloud: the sort of day when she might have met up with Barbara and gone out on what they called Parachute Patrol, roaming the woods and fields and occasionally glancing up at the sky in case a German parachute was descending. Lennie said it was daft. "There won't be a German invasion now. They're too busy invading Russia."

"We're doing a concert in aid of the Russian allies," Doreen told Rhoda. "Me and some friends: Barbara and June. And Rosie Lloyd from next door, she comes too, but she's not my friend, she just hangs around."

Rhoda looked interested. "Where are you doing it?"

"Well ... in Barbara's dad's shed at the moment." Doreen felt embarrassed. "It's a big shed. With a window. Room for people to sit around and watch. Just mums and dads, like." She could see that Rhoda had already dismissed it as kids' stuff, but she persisted. "You could join if you like. We need more people. We're having a rehearsal on Monday."

She hoped the word "rehearsal" might make the project sound more impressive.

"OK," said Rhoda. "I don't mind."

She took a box of mascara out of her dressing-table drawer and leaned forward to the mirror, brushing the stuff onto her eyelashes. Rhoda's eyelashes were white. Doreen watched them darken and thicken.

Mum would have a fit if I did that, she thought – even if I *was* thirteen.

"You have to make the best of yourself," said Rhoda. "Me mam says. You're lucky to have dark eyelashes."

Doreen had never thought about her eyelashes before. She looked at herself in the mirror: brown curly hair cut short, pale skin, grey eyes with the desired dark lashes.

"Sister Ursula says painting your face is

vanity," said Rhoda. "She says your soul is what's important, not your outward appearance. I know she's right, really, but *she* hasn't got white eyelashes."

Doreen got dressed, pulling on her baggy navy-blue knickers under cover of her nightdress.

"I've got to tidy up," she said. "But after that we could go to the pictures if you like. Or we could go to Old Works."

"What's on at the pictures?"

"*Snow White and the Seven Dwarfs*. It's good. I've seen it before."

Doreen loved cartoons. But Rhoda pulled a face. "Old Works, then," she said.

Tidying up was quick with Rhoda's help. Rhoda seemed to be expert at washing up, laying fires and making beds. She even swept the carpet and dusted.

"Mum will be pleased," said Doreen. Mum worked mornings only on Saturdays; she'd be home at midday.

"I do all that sort of thing at home," Rhoda said. "Me mam never thinks about tidying up. It's not that she's lazy," she added quickly, "only her mind's on other things. She's very talented."

Doreen was relieved to find Old Works deserted. The gangs of little boys who often infested it were not there.

"This tunnel's supposed to come out at Springhill," she said, "but I don't believe it. It's a dead-end, Lennie reckons."

The entrance to the tunnel was wide, but the roof soon sloped downwards, and Rhoda showed no interest in exploring it.

"It pongs," she said.

"I think the boys use it ... you know."

"Ugh!"

They pulled faces and giggled.

"What else is there?" asked Rhoda.

There were broken walls, remains of buildings, piles of brick rubble, all overgrown with trees and ivy. Doreen had read in a book about lost cities in the Amazon jungle; Old Works was like that, she thought.

Rhoda balanced along a stretch of wall; on one side was an eight-foot drop. "This is a great place," she said.

Doreen was gratified, and relieved; she'd been afraid Rhoda might be too grown-up for Old Works. "Come and see my favourite bit," she said, "down here."

Some steps led down into a small square room with a grating over the window. Half the roof had crumbled away and you could look up and see tree roots and ivy overhead.

"It's like a bomb site, isn't it?" she said proudly.

"Greener," said Rhoda. "Older."

"Lennie reckons it was a storeroom. We call it the Dungeon."

"There's some stuff here," said Rhoda. "In this corner."

In the dim light they caught the gleam of metal: jagged pieces of sheared-off aluminium, small round bullets, dented where they had hit the ground.

Rhoda picked up the bullets. "Shrapnel," she said. "The kids on Merseyside have tons of it."

"Hey! Leave that alone! It's ours!"

The voice came from above. A boy stood on the crumbling roof, shouting down at them: Billy Dean. More small boys appeared behind him.

"Who wants it, any road?" Doreen retorted. "Old rubbish."

Billy was clinging to a sapling. He let go and leapt into the Dungeon, bringing down a shower of earth and loose brick. He landed with a thud beside Doreen. Three other boys followed him.

"That's not rubbish," said Billy. "See that bit there? That's off a Heinkel. It's got blood on it."

"It hasn't!"

"It has! See that stain?"

Rhoda spoke up. "That's fire did that, not blood."

"It's blood!" Billy's voice was shrill.

"Blood would wash off."

He glared at her. "Know everything, don't you, Scouser?" He turned to Doreen. "Who is she, any road?"

"She's my evacuee," said Doreen. "She knows more about shrapnel than you do."

A profusion of boys' voices broke out, high-pitched, indignant. "*My* evacuee brought a whole propeller – " "My cousin gets all this stuff..." "I've got sixteen bullets – " "That's from a Messerschmidt – "

Billy Dean pulled something out of his pocket. "See that? It's a grenade."

Rhoda grabbed Doreen's arm and pushed her towards the steps. "You shouldn't mess with grenades," she said. "It could be live."

The boys crowed. "Scaredy-cats!"

Rhoda looked down at them. "You could get blown up."

Billy came to the point. "This is our den. And our stuff."

"Anyone can come here," Doreen insisted.

"Except girls and Scousers," said Billy. "So that's you two out."

Doreen and Rhoda were already moving towards the steps, but Doreen was determined to have the last word. "Smelly old dump, full of rubbish."

"Yes. Full of you. You're rubbish. Scousers are rubbish!"

Howls of laughter.

The girls retreated. "Kids!" said Rhoda contemptuously.

They went off together, a warm feeling of unity between them.

"Let's go down the High Street," said Doreen. "We can get our sweets."

She chose aniseed balls and Rhoda had pear drops and they shared them, half each. Doreen introduced Rhoda to Mrs Jennings. "This is Rhoda; she's my evacuee." She met other people she knew in the street and introduced Rhoda again. She began to feel pleased about Rhoda; she was a lot better than some of her friends' evacuees. The Palmers had those awful boys from Dudley, and Ida Jones had a girl who kept telling tales about her.

They walked home through the churchyard. Rhoda talked about her boyfriend, who was called Michael, and was a soldier, serving abroad. "We're in love," she said. "When I'm sixteen we're going to get married."

Doreen felt friendlier towards Rhoda now. She said, "My dad's buried here. Do you want to see his grave?"

Dad's headstone looked stark, although it was over a year since he had died. There were rose petals blowing around it. Doreen remembered seeing rose petals at the funeral. She had watched one fall onto the lid of the coffin and saw it crushed as the earth descended. Later there had been yellow leaves, then snow, then dandelions springing up all around. And now rose petals again.

"The flowers are dead," said Rhoda.

Last week Mum had filled a jamjar with marigolds and big white daisies; they were drooping now.

"We'll do them tomorrow," said Doreen. "We always come here on Sunday morning."

The inscription read:

THOMAS WILLIAM DYER
1888 – 1940
Rest in peace

And beneath it Mum had asked for the names of two children to be added: "George, 1923–1925" and "Joan, 1920, aged three months".

Doreen thought about those children. If they had lived they would be grown up now. In the army, or the air force, perhaps getting killed like Bobby Lee.

"Those are my mum's babies that died, and over here is Uncle Charley, and over there Uncle Arthur, and Grandad and Nan Dyer..."

"You've got a big family," said Rhoda. There was envy in her voice.

"Haven't you got any brothers or sisters?"

"No. There's only Mam and me."

"Is *your* Dad dead?"

"No."

"In the army, is he?" But even as she asked,

Doreen sensed that Rhoda didn't want to talk about her father.

Rhoda turned and began to walk towards the church. "He's away," she said, over her shoulder, "but he'll come back. After the war he'll come back and marry me mam and we'll be a proper family."

When they got home Lennie was coming in through the back garden gate, wheeling his bicycle; he only worked mornings on Saturdays.

Doreen ran up to him. "Lennie, we've been to Old Works! It was great. Rhoda likes it there, don't you, Rhoda?"

But Rhoda, with Lennie's gaze on her, shrugged, and said dismissively, "It's OK – for little kids."

Her words cast a shadow over the bright morning, spoiling it.

Doreen felt betrayed. Rhoda *had* liked it there; she was just showing off. Not that she'd got anything to show off about, seeing as her mum and dad weren't even married.

CHAPTER FOUR

On Sunday morning Rhoda went to mass, leaving the family in the kitchen, clearing breakfast.

"And how are you two getting on with Rhoda?" Mum asked.

"All right," said Doreen. And it was true. She and Rhoda had got on better than she'd expected, except for Rhoda's remark about Old Works; that still hurt. "Mum, she wears pink knickers!"

"Doreen! Not in front of Lennie!"

"Well ... I wish *I* could. And, Mum, she goes to a convent school and her teachers are nuns."

"She likes the pigeons," said Lennie.

"Has she been to the loft?"

"Yes. Last night. I told her all their names and the places they fly to. She liked them."

Doreen felt a twinge of jealousy. She didn't

know Lennie had been making friends with Rhoda.

"Rhoda's mum's a famous singer," she said.

"I saw the photo," said Mum.

"She might come and see Rhoda soon."

"Well," said Mum, "if she does come I hope she'll bring Rhoda some clothes. All she's got is those two summer frocks, and it'll be autumn soon. She'll be needing something warmer. Perhaps I should mention it when I write."

"How much do you get for having Rhoda?" Doreen asked.

"Ten and six a week."

"That's a lot."

"We won't make much on it. Not feeding a growing girl. Mind you, she's no trouble. Tidies up after herself. Always offers to help–"

"Unlike some," said Lennie, looking at Doreen.

"*You* can talk!"

"I'm bringing in money." He was proud of that, she knew.

"Mum," she began tentatively, "how much does a gold cross and chain cost – like Rhoda's?"

"I've no idea."

"I wish I had one."

"I don't really hold with crosses and that," said Mum.

"Why?"

"I just don't. We're not churchy people."

Doreen thought of Rhoda at mass. "We ought to go to chapel," she said. "We used to."

She remembered the last time she'd been. There was a visiting preacher – a woman – and the sermon wasn't as boring as usual. It was on the theme "Careless Talk Costs Lives" – the poster about spies that they all saw everywhere. Only the preacher had spoken about careless talk in everyday life; she had said that before you said anything you might regret, you should ask yourself three questions: "Is it true? Is it kind? Is it necessary?" And you should only say it if you could answer yes to at least two of them. Doreen had tested this theory, afterwards, by inventing things she might say and asking the three questions.

"I liked it – sometimes," she said. And yet she knew it wasn't really chapel she wanted to go to today. Rhoda had told her about the Catholic church, with its candles and statues and paintings, and everywhere the glint of gold and soft light. She wanted to go there.

"You could have gone to chapel, if you'd liked," said Mum. "I haven't got time. I need to change the beds and start the washing. And I could do with a bit of help. We'll get one load on the line, shall we, and then go and see your dad?"

Doreen and Lennie exchanged a glance. They both wished she wouldn't put it like that. Doreen wanted to say "Dad's dead; we can't go and see him", but when she tried the three questions on it, it only came out as true, not kind or necessary. Aunty Elsie always said that Dad had "passed over", making Doreen think of the way the flock of pigeons circled over the house. No one ever said the word dead, just as no one had ever said "dying" when Dad was ill, and yet everyone knew.

Another word she'd been thinking about came into her mind. "Mum, if your parents aren't married are you a bastard?"

Lennie snorted.

"Shut *up*, Lennie!" This was important.

Mum had tensed. "Illegitimate," she said. "There's no need to use that other word."

"I think Rhoda's illegitimate."

Mum whisked crumbs from the table. "Yes, she is, but it's not her fault. And there's no call for you to be talking about it to anyone else."

"I haven't!" She told them what Rhoda had said about her father coming home after the war.

"Is that what she says?" Mum's voice had softened. "I daresay she's had trouble from other children. People can be unkind. Let's get those sheets in the copper, Doreen. Make a start. This afternoon we're all invited up to Aunty Elsie's for tea."

Lennie grinned. "She wants to look Rhoda over."

"Oh, that's what it is," Mum agreed. "But I reckon our Rhoda will cope."

Lennie and Doreen wore their Sunday clothes to go to Aunty Elsie's. Doreen added her green ring that had come from a fair years ago. The ring was the only jewellery she possessed; she decided that from now on she'd wear it all the time, like Rhoda with her cross.

Aunty Elsie was a widow. She lived in Upper Street, across the centre of town, in a house that seemed big to Doreen. It had three bedrooms, two of them occupied by evacuee mothers and babies.

"I can't wait to see the babies!" Rhoda said, but when they arrived they found that the evacuees had been sent out for a walk; they'd be back for tea. Aunty Elsie raised her eyebrows at Mum. "Feckless – both of them. I have to push them out of the house or they'd sit around all day reading magazines. No idea about hygiene; think cooking's something you do with a tin-opener. They're all the same, these girls."

She shrugged and turned her attention to Rhoda. "So this is yours."

"This is Rhoda Kelly," said Mum. "Rhoda, this is Mrs Meadows."

Doreen had become aware, as she grew up,

that people were frightened of Aunty Elsie. Being the youngest child, and a girl, and rewarding to dress up and make clothes for, she had always been a favourite of Elsie's and had never been scared of her. But she knew her mother felt sorry for the young women billeted here. "Poor things," Doreen had overheard her saying to Phyl. "Feckless, she calls them; I remember when you were a baby and we went up to Elsie's, I used to feel feckless the minute I stepped in her door!"

Aunty Elsie was a big woman. She folded her arms across her chest and studied Rhoda.

"Well, Rhoda, and how do you like living in Culverton?" she began.

Most of the girls Doreen knew would have retreated into timid whispers under this interrogation, but not Rhoda. She spoke up clearly, and as she spoke Doreen saw her eyes flicking over Aunty Elsie and around the room, taking everything in. When Elsie had discovered her age, religion, schooling and habits, Rhoda broke in to exclaim, "This is a lovely house, Mrs Meadows. You've got such nice things; all this china – "

The dresser was stacked with china plates painted with birds and flowers. Rhoda picked one up and turned it around in her hands. Doreen had never dared to touch them and yet here was Rhoda, a stranger, walking in and handling everything. Doreen felt outraged.

"Uncle Arthur painted those, didn't he, Aunty Elsie?" she said, keen to retrieve her aunt's attention.

Uncle Arthur had been a painter at the china works and Elsie's house was full of the china seconds he had brought home. Doreen knew how proud of them Aunty Elsie was.

"He was the best painter at the works," Elsie said. "They told him that – the management. It was a great loss to the company when he passed over."

"What did he die of?" Rhoda asked, fixing Elsie with her frank blue gaze. Doreen felt apprehensive; she'd often wondered, but she'd been brought up not to ask questions like that. Strangely, Aunty Elsie didn't seem to mind. Her voice sank to a whisper as she replied, "Tuberculosis. He'd always had a weak chest, but it was the TB that took him off."

"That's a terrible thing, the TB," said Rhoda. She, too, spoke softly, and it sounded to Doreen like a grown-up speaking, as if she'd heard the phrase from her mother.

Doreen inserted herself between them. "Aunty Elsie, shall I show Rhoda round? Can I show her the piano?"

"Of course you can, love. I've got some other things in there now, as well as the piano, with all the bedrooms being full."

She went to put the kettle on, and Rhoda followed Doreen into the front room.

"Oh! A sewing machine!" exclaimed Rhoda, as if she had discovered treasure.

The sewing machine was beautiful, glossy black with gold patterning, and from it fell a swathe of blue satin material, faded in places, but shining with a soft lustre where the light caught it.

For an instant Doreen thought, It's for me! Her birthday was approaching, and in her imagination Aunty Elsie was making her a blue satin dress. Then she noticed the dress pattern that Rhoda had picked up and realized it was for an adult's ballgown.

Mum, coming in behind them, murmured, "I haven't seen material like that for a long time."

Aunty Elsie arrived with the tea tray. Her parlour might be cluttered with sewing, but she had still put out an embroidered traycloth and the best china cups.

"Is it for you, Mrs Meadows? The dress?" asked Rhoda.

"That satin?" Aunty Elsie laughed. "No. It's for Miss West up at The Laurels. Her mother bought the material before the war and never used it, and when Miss West got involved with the concert—"

"A concert?" Doreen exclaimed. "When?"

She saw Rhoda's interest quicken, too.

"Oh, not till September," said Aunty Elsie. "It's Culverton Entertainments Committee.

Miss Forrest and Mrs Miller are the organizers. I'm playing the piano, and they'll be wanting your mother to sing." She smiled at Mum, who looked anxious.

"Elsie! I haven't a thing to wear."

"Don't worry. We'll rustle something up. I'm in charge of costumes."

"Mrs Meadows." Rhoda was gazing at Aunty Elsie, shiny-eyed. "Could I help you with the costumes?"

Aunty Elsie looked surprised. "Do you like sewing, then, Rhoda?"

"I love it. And I don't always need patterns. I'm very creative, Bernadette says."

"Does she! Well, I could do with a helper," said Aunty Elsie. "Those girls and their babies – they take up such a lot of time." They heard the squeak of a gate. "And here they come, ready for their tea. Will you help me put the food out, Rhoda?"

Doreen jumped up. "I'll help, too." She followed in their wake as they went out to the kitchen. Lennie was there, testing a cooling scone. Even in wartime Elsie managed to produce cakes and scones that were almost like the real thing.

"Lennie!" said Mum.

But Elsie laughed. "You eat up, Lennie, my love. He's too thin, Lina; I've told you before. Here, Rhoda, put this cloth on the table and get some plates from the dresser."

The kitchen filled up with the women and their noisy babies. Rhoda made straight for the prettiest baby. "Oh, she's gorgeous! What's her name?"

"Christine."

"Can I hold you, Christine?" She jigged the baby on her shoulder.

The other one was screaming and had a damp nappy; Doreen avoided it. She plucked at Aunty Elsie's sleeve. "Can I sing in the concert, like Mum?"

"Oh, it's not for children, Doreen, love. This is an adult's concert. Children won't be performing this time." It wasn't fair, Doreen thought. But Mum, who had overheard, said, "You've got your own concert that you're doing, haven't you, Doreen? With Barbara and June? You'll be singing in that."

"It's not the same," said Doreen.

"When I grow up," Rhoda said that night, "I'm going to have my own house, and everything nice, like at your Aunty Elsie's."

Doreen was still feeling jealous at the way Rhoda had got on so well with Aunty Elsie. "I've never known Elsie take to anyone outside the family the way she has Rhoda," Mum had said afterwards. And Doreen had felt pushed out; she'd been her aunt's favourite for as long as she could remember.

She said sourly, "Mum says Aunty Elsie's is

nice because she hasn't got children."

"Oh, but I shall have children! Two at least. Twins."

Twins! Doreen was drawn in, in spite of herself. She wanted twins, too. Amanda and Angela. Or Isla and Irene...

"You know that concert they're doing?" said Rhoda. "I'd like to be in that. To sing."

"Well, you can't." Doreen couldn't keep the satisfaction out of her voice. "It's for grown-ups only. Didn't Aunty Elsie tell you?"

CHAPTER FIVE

"I can see it up your sleeve," said June.

Doreen sighed, and pulled out the scarf. It wasn't easy being a magician. Marbles rolled on the floor and cards slipped from her fingers, revealing their secrets. Maybe she should just sing – she was better at that. But they needed a lot of acts and there weren't many people to go round. June was going to juggle with tennis balls, and she had brought along a rabbit which she said could perform tricks. Barbara – who was easily embarrassed – had been persuaded against her will to do a spoof cookery demonstration: how to make a pudding out of chopped newspaper, tea leaves and water. Rosie Lloyd was tap-dancing – not because she could dance but because June's outgrown tap shoes fitted her.

And now there was Rhoda. Doreen had wondered, this morning, whether she was right to have invited Rhoda to join them. But Rhoda was older, and her mother was on the stage. Maybe she could give this show the professionalism it needed.

"I used to know a magician," said Rhoda. "Friend of me mam's. It's all done with sleight of hand."

"I know that," retorted Doreen. "Only my hands aren't sleight."

"He said you have to get their attention away – so they're looking at the box while you're slipping the scarf up your sleeve."

"I can watch the box and the scarf at the same time," said June.

You would, thought Doreen. She was going off June.

"Did this magician teach you how to do any tricks?" she asked Rhoda.

"No. He couldn't. They're all in this guild, The Magic Circle, and they're not allowed to tell how they do it. It's against the rules."

"Well, I could see the scarf," said June, "and I could see you changing the cards over in the other trick."

Barbara said, "I expect the mums and dads will pretend they didn't see."

"But I want it to be *right*," said Doreen. It was especially important now; she didn't want to look a fool in front of Rhoda.

"Are you going to sing for us, then, Rhoda?" asked June. "You said you would."

Rhoda walked into the centre of the shed and faced them. "I'll sing 'Yours'," she said.

As she started to sing, Doreen saw Barbara and June exchange astonished glances. Doreen could sing, but not like this. Doreen sang like a child, but Rhoda's voice was much fuller, and she sang as if she really meant it, with gestures and expressions just like Vera Lynn's. The others burst out clapping as the song came to an end.

Doreen felt pleased – Rhoda would add such a lot to the show. But she was jealous, too, at being outshone. Until now she had been the one who was best at singing, the one with all the ideas and the one who did most of the organizing. But Rhoda was already beginning to take over. "I used to tap dance," she said. She began to dance alongside Rosie, encouraging her to swing her arms and loosen her knees, and suddenly Rosie didn't seem so hopeless after all; she was dancing quite well, though not with Rhoda's style.

"We need a curtain," Rhoda decided next. "And music – or a drum roll. To announce the start."

"A dustbin lid!" said Doreen. "And a stick."

"Yes!" Barbara fetched them, and Rhoda produced an impressive drum roll, rising to a crescendo.

"I want to do that!" said June.

"We'll take turns," said Rhoda.

She was in charge now. Barbara was sent indoors to ask about curtains. Rosie was allowed to practise the drum roll.

"When are we putting on this performance?" Rhoda asked, and Doreen felt foolish, realizing that she hadn't thought; the rehearsing had seemed to be all that mattered.

"We could do it on Saturday," she said, "in the afternoon."

"We'll need posters. And tickets."

"I'll do them." Doreen liked doing things like that.

"I'll help," said Rhoda.

Doreen felt her resentment of Rhoda rising again. It's my concert, she thought, my idea; they're my friends, not yours.

She turned away and fondled the rabbit. She liked the rabbit, even though it had failed to perform any of its tricks. They had rabbits at home, but Doreen ignored them; she dared not get fond of a rabbit she was going to have to eat. Clearly June was less sentimental.

The group broke up at tea-time, and Doreen and Rhoda walked home together. Rhoda was full of the concert; she'd taken over the organization of it and seemed quite unaware of Doreen's feelings.

On Tuesday morning a postcard with a view of the Mersey ferry came from Rhoda's mother. It was dated two weeks earlier and had been forwarded from Rhoda's previous billet, via Miss Wingfield. The message was brief: "Show going well – full house every night. Be good. All my love, M."

Mum said, "I'll have to write to your mother."

"Miss Wingfield will have told her I've moved," said Rhoda.

"But I'll write any road. It's only polite."

Doreen was impressed by the picture postcard. They'd only once had one before: from Phyl when she went on a day-trip to Barmouth; but she was back before it arrived, so it wasn't the same.

"Mam always sends me cards," said Rhoda. "I've kept them all. I'll show you later."

"Does Michael write to you?"

"Oh, yes."

But from Rhoda's look Doreen realized that she had no chance of being shown *those* letters.

Mum was off to work. She tied a headscarf into a turban and tucked in her hair. "Can you girls tidy up?"

Doreen would have left the tidying-up until the last minute and then done it half-heartedly. But Rhoda set to as soon as Mum had gone, clearing out the ash from the fire, washing the dishes, making the beds. She did everything properly, as if she enjoyed it. Doreen's resentment grew. Rhoda was just trying to get in with Mum, she thought.

She left Rhoda sweeping the floor and went upstairs to find some paper and make a start on the tickets and posters. She'd get them done, she decided, before Rhoda could take over.

There wasn't much clean paper; only paper bags, too crumpled for posters. Doreen smoothed one out and started anyway, making a border of flowers and leaves and writing SUMMER SHOW in capitals in the centre.

Rhoda came in. "Oh! What are you doing?"

Reluctantly Doreen told her. "But the paper's no good. I'll have to ask Barbara for some – her dad has invoices and things."

She put the paper and pencil on the dressing-table, hoping Rhoda would go away. But Rhoda didn't. She said, "We could plan it first."

"Plan?" Doreen had never thought of planning anything.

Rhoda retrieved Doreen's poster. "This is OK. But you need heavier lettering." She turned it over and wrote SUMMER SHOW in blocked three-dimensional characters. Immediately it began to look like a real poster; Doreen felt pleased and thwarted at the same time.

"Venue," wrote Rhoda, "The Garden Shed, 26 High Street, Culverton."

"'Starring.'" Doreen reached for the pencil, but Rhoda held on.

"'Starring'," said Rhoda. "Who should come first?"

They eyed each other.

Doreen had an inspiration. "Alphabetical," she said. A quick run-through had showed her that this way she would be first legitimately; and, even more satisfying, June Wilkins would be last.

"I don't know the surnames," said Rhoda.

Doreen reached for the pencil again, but Rhoda evaded her, turned the paper over and began jotting them down: "Kelly; Dyer; what's Barbara's?"

"Lee," said Doreen. "And there's Lloyd and Wilkins."

"You're first, then, and I'm second, then Barbara Lee..."

Rhoda wrote the names at an angle, so that they seemed to interlock, and she drew six-pointed stars in between them. It was better than anything Doreen would have thought of.

"Admission," said Rhoda. "How much should we charge?"

"Fourpence?"

"Sixpence."

"All right."

"And we must put what it's in aid of: the Red Army."

She wrote, "In aid of our gallant Russian comrades," and drew a soldier in a greatcoat and Russian hat.

She could draw better than Doreen, too.

That night, while Rhoda was upstairs, Mum wrote to Rhoda's mother. Doreen had to help her. "I can never think what to put," said Mum.

Even starting was difficult. Should she begin "Dear Anne-Marie" or "Dear Mrs Kelly" or... Doreen realized that Mum couldn't bring herself to mention the third, more accurate possibility: "Dear Miss Kelly".

They decided on "Mrs Kelly".

"Dear Mrs Kelly, I expect Miss Wingfield has told you that Rhoda is now billeted with me." She crossed out "billeted" and wrote "staying". "It's friendlier, like." She chewed the end of the pen. "What else shall I say?"

"Say she does good posters but she's taking over everything and we hope she'll be going home soon!" Doreen burst out.

"Oh, Doreen!" Mum put down her pen. "I don't think you've *tried* to like her."

"I have!" Doreen felt she'd tried hard. Her eyes brimmed with tears. "Mum, she's bossy."

"Well ... so are you."

"But I'm not *horrible*!" Doreen said, and realized, even before Mum's lips twitched, that at the moment she was being just that; reluctantly she gave way to laughter while the tears ran down her face.

"No, you're not," said Mum, composing

her face. "So please help me with this letter. 'Settled' – shall we say that?"

"Yes." But she added sulkily, "Only I still wish she'd go home."

Mum ignored this. "'Rhoda has settled in. She is well and happy. We will be pleased to see you if you wish to call –' Does that sound all right? Oh, dear: I ought to ask for money for clothes, but it seems rude, doesn't it, in the first letter? Perhaps in a P.S...."

She wrote, "Yours sincerely, A. Dyer (Mrs)" and added "P.S. I don't like to mention it but Rhoda needs new shoes and a coat for autumn." She turned to Doreen. "Do you think I should put that in?"

"Yes!" said Doreen. "Rhoda says the shoes are hurting."

This was true, but it had also occurred to Doreen that if Rhoda got new shoes she might get the old ones.

Mum read the letter through, worrying that it should have been longer, that it might not be impressive enough for someone who called herself Anne-Marie and was on the stage.

"It's all right," Doreen assured her, and Mum copied it out neatly and put it in an envelope addressed to "Mrs M. Kelly, 72 Furnival Buildings, Crown Street, Bootle".

Perhaps she'll come and see us soon, Doreen thought. She longed to meet Anne-Marie.

CHAPTER SIX

"I'm going out," said Lennie. "Get some air."

It was a fine evening and he'd been underground all day.

"Take the girls," said Mum. "I heard there's a hedge full of raspberries over Brick Kiln Lane. You could pick me some."

They took some paper bags and went out.

The evening was golden. Long shadows lay across the street. Women stood at their front doors, arms crossed, gossiping. Rosie Lloyd and the Richards children were playing hopscotch on the pavement.

Doreen saw that Rosie had spotted her and was beginning to detach herself from the hopscotch. "Quick," she said. "Let's get away." From the corner of her eye she saw Rosie run after them, hesitate, and drift back to her game.

Lennie led the girls on a short cut across

fields. They skirted the edge of Old Works – where boys' voices floated up, bird-like, on the still air – then crossed Old Hall Lane and climbed a stile into the fields. Lennie was quiet – shy because of Rhoda. If she hadn't been there, he and Doreen would have been sparring with each other. It was Rhoda who talked, asking questions, always of Lennie, what this crop was, when it would be harvested, what work did he do in the pit, did they have ponies, wasn't it horrible working in the dark all the time?

"I shan't stay there," said Lennie. "When the war's over I'm going to try and get a job in Birmingham, in a drawing office."

"Lennie's really good at drawing," said Doreen.

"No, I'm not." He sounded irritated. "But I could learn."

They came to a field of cows. As they climbed over the stile the cows began moving towards them. Rhoda hesitated.

"They won't hurt you," Lennie said.

But Rhoda didn't move.

"Walk the other side of me," said Lennie. "No – don't hurry. Just walk."

The cows came close: bulky bodies, snorting puffs of breath. Lennie waved a hand at the cows, and the leaders, startled, shifted back a step. "See, they're scared of us. They're just nosy."

"I don't like them," said Rhoda.

"City girl," teased Lennie.

He and Doreen walked either side of her.

The next field was full of some fodder crop, knee-high with limp leaves and yellow flowers. It brushed pollen onto Doreen's blue frock.

"Rabbit! Look!" They saw the white scut vanishing into the hedge. Lennie pretended to shoot it. He had lost his shyness and was showing off for Rhoda's benefit.

"I can see the raspberries!" said Doreen. She ran ahead, through the gap in the hedge and into the cornfield that bordered Brick Kiln Lane.

The raspberries hung in thick arching clusters. No one had found this side of the hedge yet. The fruit was soft red, deepening to crimson, so ripe it fell at a touch. It was too soft to keep; they ate greedily.

"I'd never had them till the war," said Rhoda. "Only in jam. Didn't like them at first."

"We'd better save some," said Lennie.

Doreen began filling one of the paper bags. Lennie and Rhoda worked together, Lennie holding a bag open, Rhoda dropping the fruit in.

"Hold one for me, Lennie," said Doreen. It was awkward trying to hold the bag open while you picked the fruit. But Lennie said, "You're doing all right," and moved on down the hedge.

They walked home laden. The sun was a pink glow in the west and dusk was gathering beneath the hedge and under the knots of trees. The cows were gone from their field. Lennie teased Rhoda, and she laughed. The two of them walked ahead, and Doreen heard Rhoda telling Lennie about Merseyside, and the bombing, and then they got onto the war and the reasons for it, and Lennie talked about his friend Howard who worked at Springhill pit; Howard was a conscientious objector and he'd volunteered to work in the mine rather than join the forces.

"But it's all the same, isn't it?" asked Rhoda. "I mean, he's helping us win the war."

Doreen, trailing behind, felt left out. Lennie never talked to her – not properly, about sensible things, only to tease. And lately, since he'd been at work, he'd had no time for her at all. He was too tired in the evenings to play marbles or jacks or ludo, and he didn't always want to go to Saturday morning pictures either; he preferred to be outside. He spent a lot of time out on his bike, with his friend Martin. Doreen suspected that although they pretended to be grown-up, they played the same sort of games as she did with Barbara: looking for spies, and parachutists, and military storage depots. "Can I come?" she'd asked, but they didn't want her around.

When they reached Old Works, the children were gone. It was almost dark.

"Let's go to the Dungeon," said Lennie.

"Oh, yes!" Rhoda was enthusiastic.

Doreen thought of the Dungeon, black and secret under the trees. Lennie knew she was scared of the dark. "It's late," she said.

"You go home, then."

But Doreen wouldn't. She followed them, stumbling over the uneven ground, until they reached the entrance to the storeroom, deep in its well of darkness.

"Can't see a thing," laughed Lennie. His foot struck against something metallic.

"The kids brought shrapnel here," said Doreen. "Billy Dean and that lot. They had a grenade. Rhoda was scared, weren't you, Rhoda?"

She was scared herself, now, afraid of the darkness that pressed against her eyes as she entered the underground room, and angry with Lennie for making her come here. His shirt-sleeve gleamed white in the darkness; she grabbed it and held on.

Lennie moved further in, and Doreen was pulled with him. The light from the tiny barred window showed up faint outlines, but the corners of the room were black.

"It'd be a good place, this, to hide out," said Lennie. "A spy – "

"Or a German prisoner on the run," said

Rhoda. *She* wasn't frightened.

Doreen pressed against Lennie. "I don't like it here."

Lennie took pity on her. "Let's go home. Mum will be wondering."

Doreen got some paper from Barbara, and the three girls spent a morning designing posters and tickets. Barbara didn't seem to mind being bossed by Rhoda; she was happy to be told what to do. But Doreen did two of the posters and deliberately made them different from Rhoda's, although she copied the blocked lettering. Barbara cut out and printed the tickets. Rhoda had decided that more rehearsals were needed, so the date was put forward to the Saturday after next.

When the posters were finished they distributed them around the town: one in each of the children's houses, one in the butcher's shop and one in Jennings' sweet shop.

The extra rehearsals did little to improve the performances. June still insisted she could see through Doreen's magic tricks, and Rosie still couldn't dance. The rabbit escaped. Doreen was glad. She thought of it out in the fields with the wild rabbits, its white scut bounding in the distance like the one they'd seen on Brick Kiln Lane. Lennie said, "It'll just get shot instead of having its neck broken," but Doreen thought that at least it had a chance. Besides, it got June into trouble with her mum, who hadn't known she'd been bringing it.

Meanwhile, plans for the adults' concert were going ahead. "What shall I sing?" asked Mum. Doreen suggested her own favourites: "The Lark in the Clear Air" and "Somewhere Over the Rainbow".

Aunty Elsie began making costumes, and Rhoda spent several days helping her cut out and pin and tack. Doreen went, too, the first time – she'd always liked going to Aunty Elsie's. They let her pin some of the pieces together, but she felt dissatisfied; Rhoda was so much better at everything than she was.

The next day she went to Barbara's instead, and they roamed the woods and fields, playing a game of Doreen's invention: they were spies, parachuted into occupied France to help the Resistance. They hid in the undergrowth and watched the boys with their war games and bits of shrapnel, and pretended they were watching Germans.

That evening, when Doreen came back from Barbara's at tea-time, she heard singing in the kitchen as she approached the back door, the opening words of "Somewhere Over the Rainbow."

Mum and Rhoda.

Doreen stood still. She couldn't bring herself to go in. She had always sung with Mum, ever since she was two or three and Mum had taught her nursery rhymes; and then songs like "She'll Be Coming Round the Mountain" and "Dashing Away With a Smoothing Iron". And now Mum was singing with Rhoda. She listened to Rhoda's husky, grown-up contralto and knew she would never be as good as that; Mum would always prefer to sing with Rhoda now.

She ran down the garden path to the pigeon loft and went inside. The birds rustled on their perches. Doreen sniffed back tears. I'm being stupid, she thought. She found Dad's old jacket still hanging on the hook behind the door and rubbed her face against it, but it only smelt of dust and grain; Dad had gone. Doreen had never taken much interest in the birds, but now they were a soft, comforting presence. She sat on Dad's chair and let the sound of their cooing soothe her.

The door opened, making her jump: Lennie, come to feed them.

"What's up?" he asked.

"Nothing." Doreen rubbed a hand across her face.

"You know, if you don't get on with Rhoda you should tell Mum."

"I have. She doesn't care." She glowered at him. "*You* seem to like her."

Lennie picked up a pigeon and examined its wing feathers. "She makes you like her – the way she's interested in everything. But I can see it would be different for you."

Doreen nodded. Rhoda was like a river that had flowed into all her space.

"They've stopped singing now," said Lennie. He smiled. "It's safe to go in."

"*There* you are!" said Mum. "Rhoda's upstairs. We've been having a sing-song."

"Rhoda sings better than me," said Doreen.

"Different," amended Mum.

"She sounds like the wireless."

"To be honest" – Mum lowered her voice – "I prefer a child to sound like a child. Rhoda's a bit ... precocious." And then she looked guilty, as if she regretted saying that to Doreen.

But Doreen was glad she had.

Precocious.

She liked that word.

The letter to Rhoda's mother was returned, marked "Gone away".

"She must have moved," said Rhoda. "She's always moving." She seemed unconcerned.

"But doesn't she let you know her new address?"

"You could send it to the theatre."

Doreen sensed her mother's disapproval as she addressed another envelope. "I'd better take you to Bensons'," she said to Rhoda, "and buy you some new shoes. We can post this on the way."

She bought Rhoda a pair of plimsolls. The Dyers always wore plimsolls unless Mum managed to get a pair of shoes at a jumble sale. "They'll do for a few months," she said.

Doreen inherited the black patent shoes. They were too big, but she wore them anyway, with insoles and her thickest socks.

Rosie Lloyd came round that night, wanting Doreen to play.

"I can't," said Doreen. "We're rehearsing."

She and Rhoda had chosen their songs. Doreen was singing "Run, Rabbit, Run" and Rhoda, "We'll Meet Again".

"I'll listen," said Rosie. She tried to sidle into the house, but Doreen shooed her away. "Go and practise your dancing."

And Rosie did. They heard the lonely *tap, tap* of her second-hand shoes echoing in the passage between the houses. Doreen felt mean. But there were only two days left before the Grand Summer Show; she didn't have time for Rosie.

Rhoda missed the last two rehearsals; she was at Aunty Elsie's making costumes. Doreen was surprised and slightly offended that she hadn't put the rehearsals first, but on the other hand it gave Doreen a chance to take charge, and it wasn't as if Rhoda herself needed to practise.

Then, on the Friday, the day before the show, Rhoda said casually, "Oh, I can't come tomorrow, Doreen. I'm going out with Lennie and Martin. We're taking the pigeons for a toss."

Doreen stared. "But it's the performance!"

"We'll do it on Sunday."

"We can't. June's going to her aunt's. And Mrs Lee always spends hours at the cemetery, Sundays; she won't come."

"Next week, then."

"Rhoda, the others are already fed up – they wanted to do it last week. And it's on all the posters."

"Well, do it without me; I don't mind."

But Doreen knew it wouldn't be the same now without Rhoda.

"You don't *have* to go out with Lennie and Martin," she said furiously.

"I do. I promised. And it's the only day. I'm sorry, Doreen, honestly."

Doreen stormed downstairs and ripped the poster from the door. She went out and called over the garden fence to Rosie to take her poster down. Then she slammed the garden gate and ran to Barbara's.

Barbara was comforting and sympathetic, but she didn't care the way Doreen did.

"I *hate* Rhoda!" said Doreen.

"She is a bit bossy," agreed Barbara. "We could do it any road, Doreen. We don't have to have Rhoda. I know she's a good singer and that, but it was more fun before."

Doreen and Barbara had been best friends for ages. Doreen realized that Barbara had been missing their togetherness.

"If you want to get your own back, do it without her," said Barbara.

But Doreen couldn't. Her enthusiasm had gone. She was in a wrecking mood. She went home and complained bitterly to Mum.

"She shouldn't have done it," Mum agreed. "Trouble is, she's older than you; she's got other interests. I expect it all seemed a bit young, with kids like Rosie in it."

"Then why did she come and take over in the first place?" retorted Doreen.

Lennie came into the room – and took the brunt of her temper.

"It's not my fault!" he insisted. "I just asked her; she never said about the show."

"She wouldn't."

"I'll tell her she can't come." But he looked unwilling.

"Don't bother," said Doreen.

CHAPTER SEVEN

Rhoda and Lennie left at twelve the next morning, as soon as Lennie got home from work.

"'Bye, Doreen," said Rhoda in a small voice. She looked sheepish. Doreen guessed Mum had had a word with her last night.

"Have a good time," she said sarcastically.

Mum sighed and shook her head. She began clearing the table.

Doreen heard Lennie and Rhoda talking as they walked across the yard. Then she heard the sound of the shed door opening. She sprang to her feet.

"My bike!" she said.

"Doreen – " Mum began. But Doreen was already out in the yard.

Lennie's bicycle was propped up against the shed wall and he was bringing out the other one: a lady's, with a basket on the front.

Doreen threw herself at him. "She's not having my bike!"

"It's not yours. It's Mary's." Lennie felt the tyres: squashy; he unclipped the pump.

"It's mine for now."

"Yours and Mum's," said Lennie. He was pumping steadily.

"I asked your mam," said Rhoda.

Doreen glared at her. "You never asked me! And you're not having it." She grabbed at the handlebars, knocking Lennie off balance.

"For heaven's sake, Doreen," he shouted, "don't be so babyish!"

Mum had come out. "Doreen, I told Rhoda she could take the bike. It's Mary's bike, not yours. Now leave Lennie alone."

Doreen gave the bicycle a hard shove towards Lennie and ran inside.

Everybody was against her. She hated them all. She stormed upstairs and into her bedroom. The two beds confronted her; hers unmade, Rhoda's neatly covered with its floral quilt.

She hated Rhoda.

She began to drag out the screen from behind the dressing-table. Mum came up, alarmed by the noise.

"What *are* you doing?

"I want the screen up."

"You're being silly."

"I'm not!" Doreen was close to tears. She

got the screen into place and retreated behind it, to her own bed.

Mum followed her. "*I* told Rhoda she could have the bike. I know she was wrong to let you down, but refusing her the bike wouldn't have made any difference."

"It might have stopped her going."

"And how would she have felt, then? She still wouldn't have wanted to join in with you."

"It's not fair," said Doreen. "She gets everything."

"She doesn't. I treat you all the same."

"I didn't mean that. I meant ... people. Lennie. Aunty Elsie."

"Elsie does seem to like her," Mum agreed.

"She used to like me."

"Oh, Doreen! She loves you. You can love more than one person, you know. It isn't rationed – not like butter."

Doreen plucked at the patchwork quilt – the one Aunty Elsie had made her. "That Rhoda – she pushes in," she muttered.

"Perhaps no one takes much notice of her back home," suggested Mum. "If you could share Lennie and Aunty Elsie with her, while she's here... It won't be for ever." She stood up briskly. "Why don't you go and see Barbara?" Mum liked Barbara. "You might even feel like doing the show. I'll turn up any road. I've got my ticket."

"I don't know," said Doreen.

But she went to Barbara's. Barbara was sitting on her back doorstep shelling peas. Her cat, Tiggy, was on her lap, struggling to get comfortable and nudging the colander out of his way.

"Get him off me, Dor," said Barbara.

Doreen picked up Tiggy and held him on her own lap as she sat down, but he was soon back on Barbara, pressing and purring.

"I'll have the colander." Doreen popped open a pea pod and brushed the row of peas into the bowl. She tasted one. It was crunchy and fresh.

"I can't stop eating them," said Barbara.

The sun was warm on their heads. Doreen popped pea pods and stroked Tiggy and ate fresh peas and slowly the anger melted out of her. Barbara didn't talk much except to say, "Ugh! A wormy one!" or "Get *off*, Tiggy!" But after a while she asked, "Are we doing the show, then?"

"Yes, let's do it. We don't need her."

"Will Rosie come?"

Doreen pulled a face. "Bound to. I told her it was cancelled but that wouldn't stop Rosie."

"June's still coming. But her mum won't let her bring another rabbit."

Doreen was stroking Tiggy. She looked up, and smiled. "I've got an idea. About your cookery demonstration."

Barbara hung her head. "It's awful."

"No, it's not. But listen."

The garden shed was full. Barbara's mother was there; and June's. Mum had brought Mrs Richards from up the road and Miss Wingfield, who'd been passing by. There was an old man, Mr Ross – a neighbour of the Lees – and his collie dog, and Barbara's sister Sylvia who was on shift-work and had her curlers in, ready for bed. Doreen, getting her props together behind the screen which Mrs Lee had provided, totted up in her head: three and six already, and then there was to be the raffle.

She turned to Rosie. "Will your mum come?"

Rosie wiped her nose on the back of her hand. She always had a runny nose. "She never goes anywhere," she said.

Doreen thought of Mrs Lloyd, moaning to Mum over the washing lines about the state of her insides. Nobody had much time for Mrs Lloyd – or Rosie.

I ought to be kinder to Rosie, Doreen thought. But it was hard.

Doreen had swiftly rearranged the programme with Barbara. June was on first with her juggling. That pleased June, who felt honoured, but Doreen knew it was better to be last; she intended to finish the show herself with two songs.

The audience was restless. "Oi!" called old Mr Ross. "Let's be having you then!" A chorus of giggled "Shushes!" from the women followed this.

"Let's start," whispered Doreen.

She held up the dustbin lid and produced the drum roll. The dog began to bark. Doreen darted out from behind the screen and announced, "High Street Entertainments Committee presents a Grand Summer Show!"

June did her juggling act. She was good, but she did drop one ball; the collie made a dash for it. Doreen, peeping through a crack in the screen, saw the dog sitting in front of June, eager for another one.

June was pink with suppressed laughter when she came off. "I nearly dropped the lot."

Doreen went out again. "Miss Rosie Lloyd!"

Rosie was lost without Rhoda. She had done all her rehearsals with Rhoda directing her, and now she blundered through the routine, ended in a brief flurry of taps, and came off looking bewildered. Doreen heard the audience clapping. She said, "That was good, Rosie!" and was rewarded with one of Rosie's rare smiles.

Doreen's magic was next; but there were problems backstage. Doreen could hear a persistent miaowing: Tiggy, who was being restrained in a box. The dog began to growl, and Doreen was aware of Mrs Lee and Sylvia whispering together, "What's Barbara *doing* to that cat?"

Doreen's problems with the scarf and the marbles went largely unnoticed; far more interesting were the increasingly frantic miaows and sounds of scrabbling and shushing behind the screen.

Doreen realized that things were getting out of hand. She cut her act short and announced the cookery demonstration.

Barbara brought on a table, a mixing bowl and spoon, a pie dish, and some cream-coloured cloth. The back stage miaowing was muffled now; Doreen held Tiggy while she watched through the crack. Barbara was blushing bright pink, but she managed to say her lines. "In this time of austerity we cooks have to make do with whatever comes to hand. Rabbit is not always available, but have you thought of tempting the family with cat? Cats are abundant and very tasty. I will now demonstrate how to make a nourishing cat pie."

This was Doreen's cue to release Tiggy, who shot onstage. The collie broke into a frenzy of barking, and Mr Ross grabbed his collar. "Steady on, old lad," he said. "You can have him when he's cooked."

"First, catch your cat," puffed Barbara, as she chased around between the chairs. She pounced and caught Tiggy and brought him to the table, where she wrapped him in the cream cloth to look like pastry and put him in the pie dish. Tiggy was outraged. Bits of him kept emerging from the pastry: an ear, a paw, two paws, his head and shoulders. The audience rocked with laughter.

Tiggy burst free of his packaging and hurtled backstage. The dog was frantic. Barbara, no longer embarrassed, smiled at her audience and said, "On the other hand, you may find that a leek and potato pie is far less trouble..."

Doreen was calming Tiggy behind the screen. Now she had to sing. As she had guessed, the audience was in tears of laughter, so she began with a funny one: "The Quarter Master's Stores".

"There was Brenda, Brenda, fixing her suspender
In the stores, in the stores..."

As she sang, she heard her mother saying in a horrified voice to Mrs Lee, "I don't know where she learned this one..."

Rhoda had been going to finish the show with "We'll Meet Again", and Doreen had thought: *I'll* sing it; that'll teach her. But it didn't feel right, and at the last moment she went back to her original choice, "Run, Rabbit, Run."

The audience loved it. Doreen saw them all

swaying as they joined in and knew she'd done the right thing: she didn't have to try to be Rhoda.

Mr Ross won the raffle: a bottle of Aunty Elsie's elderflower wine. The girls totted up. "Three and six, plus four and eight for the raffle: that's eight shillings and twopence."

Doreen gave the money to Miss Wingfield, who knew where it should be sent.

The group began to break up. Sylvia went to bed, and Miss Wingfield drove off in her car. Mr Ross went home with his dog and his bottle of wine. But everyone else stayed and sat on the grass, drinking tea.

The girls played jacks. Doreen tossed the pieces, caught three on the back of her hand, tossed again, and picked up one while the other was in the air. She was deft at this, and her turn lasted a long time. When June took over the pieces Doreen moved back, and overheard her mother saying, "... a bit of a tiff..."

She's talking about me and Rhoda, Doreen thought.

Mum and Mrs Lee spoke in low voices, their heads close together. Doreen listened.

"... never a word from her ... returned marked 'gone away'..."

"You'd think she'd get in touch."

"... nothing new. Miss Wingfield says she never visited ... only child ... must be an encumbrance..."

"It makes you wonder..."

The voices sank lower, but Doreen caught the words "father" and "unsettled", and "drifting".

Mum leaned back and her voice came more clearly. "Well, it's not for us to criticize, but..."

"Doreen!" Barbara interrupted. "It's your turn again."

Rhoda and Lennie came home at six o'clock, sunburnt and tired.

Lennie said, "We went right over to Wendon."

"You must be starving," said Mum.

Rhoda chatted to Mum as they got the dinner; she avoided Doreen's eye.

Later, upstairs in their room, Doreen said, "We did that show – in case you're interested."

Rhoda went pink. "Did it go well?"

"Great. Everyone enjoyed it. We made eight and twopence." She would have liked to share with Rhoda the fun that her cat-pie idea had created and tell her which songs she'd sung, but she couldn't; she and Rhoda might be on speaking terms but they weren't friends.

Rhoda fiddled with her hair slide. She said, "I'm sorry I let you down."

"I suppose Mum told you to say that?"

Rhoda turned with a flash of anger. "Look, I've said I'm sorry."

"It's OK," said Doreen. "We didn't need you."

CHAPTER EIGHT

"I'm going to Aunty Elsie's after mass," said Rhoda. "Do you want to come too?"

She spoke from behind the screen. It was a week since their quarrel, but Doreen still wanted the screen in place. She was determined to stay angry with Rhoda.

"I'm not bothered," she said.

Rhoda's bedsprings creaked as she sat up. She'd be unpinning her hair and brushing it into curls. "I'm taking the babies out if it's fine. Their mams said I could."

Doreen wanted to go. She wanted to push the babies out in the second-hand pram the WVS had provided. She wanted to see Aunty Elsie and be made a fuss of. But Rhoda was trying to get round her, and she wasn't having it.

She got up. Behind the blackout curtain she could hear rain pattering. All week the weather had been wet and cold, trapping them indoors. She and Rhoda had been unable to avoid each other. Doreen had taken to reading more than usual, partly because she liked reading, but also because it was a way of shutting Rhoda out. She had noticed that Rhoda never read books. When Doreen and Lennie were both reading, Rhoda would pace about restlessly, trying to catch the eye of one of them, eager to break in and talk.

Rhoda went off early to church, wearing the blue raincoat Mum had bought for her at the WI jumble sale. Anne-Marie still hadn't sent any money for clothes, and there had been no reply to Mum's letter, not even a postcard.

Doreen remembered Rhoda's collection of postcards. They had looked at them all one evening, not long after she first came, and Doreen had been fascinated by the photographs of different towns and the romantic-sounding postmarks: Blackpool, Southport, Colwyn Bay, Rhyl. There was never much written on the back: "Lovely audiences, mainly servicemen, full houses"; and once, back in May, "Bombing all night. Fires, searchlights, sirens. You should see the bags under my eyes! Hope you're being a good girl. Love and kisses, M."

"She puts *M*," Rhoda had said. "She doesn't like 'Mam'."

For the first time Doreen wondered whether

Rhoda minded about her mother not writing. I'd mind, she thought. But perhaps it was different if your mother was famous.

And other people wrote to Rhoda: Sister Ursula, from her old school, and Bernadette O'Farrell, who did Anne-Marie's dressmaking. Not Rhoda's boyfriend, though.

"Mum," she said, "Rhoda's boyfriend never writes to her."

Mum was filling the copper and sorting the dirty washing into heaps on the floor.

"If she's got a boyfriend," she said.

"She has! I told you: he's twenty-two and he used to live next door to them in Anfield and he's in the army."

"Oh, I'm sure he exists," agreed Mum. "I just wonder ... you mustn't take everything Rhoda says literally. I mean, he may not think of her as his girlfriend."

Doreen was puzzled. Rhoda had been so positive.

"Perhaps his letters aren't getting through," she said. But Jim, Phyl's husband, was in the army, and Phyl was always getting letters from him.

Mum put the wireless on. It was time for the Sunday Service and she liked the hymns.

"O worship the King all-glorious above;
O gratefully sing His power and His love..."

They both joined in.

Doreen wanted to smile and sing at the same time. She was happy; she had Mum to herself and they were singing together again.

When the prayers started she said, "Let's practise your songs for the concert."

Rehearsals for the concert were already underway, with the church hall booked for the sixth of September. Mum was planning to sing "It's a Lovely Day Tomorrow" and "Somewhere Over the Rainbow". She switched the wireless off and they began.

"I *wish* I could be in the concert too," said Doreen.

She longed to be part of it all. Mum would be singing, Aunty Elsie playing the piano, and she wanted nothing so much as to be up there with them on the stage. She'd wear her Sunday dress and Rhoda's black patent shoes, and perhaps Phyl would lend her that hair slide with the twinkly bits...

Mum was sympathetic. "But Miss Forrest says if she starts letting children in she'll get all the little ones. She wants it to be professional."

"I am *quite* professional," said Doreen.

At dinner-time Rhoda came in, wet through, her hair in rats' tails. She hadn't been able to take the babies out. Doreen was glad.

It rained all day. After dinner Lennie went to the pigeon loft and Rhoda turned to

Doreen. "Do you want to play something? Chess?"

Doreen liked chess, and Rhoda knew it.

"It's OK," said Doreen. "I told Rosie she could come round."

It wasn't true, but, having said it, Doreen felt obliged to make it true. She endured an afternoon with Rosie, playing snakes and ladders because Rosie wasn't clever enough for chess. Rhoda went out to the loft to talk to Lennie, and later Doreen heard her chatting and laughing with Mum upstairs as they put clean sheets on the bed. She wondered, jealously, what they were finding to talk about.

Rosie, once in, was always difficult to get rid of; but Doreen was ruthless. "You'll have to go now – we're having our tea."

Rosie wiped her hand across her nose. "I can stay to tea."

"No, you can't."

She hustled Rosie out into the yard.

"We could have given Rosie a bit of tea," Mum said later.

"I don't want her here."

"You shouldn't ask her round, then."

Doreen didn't reply. She suspected that Mum knew why she had asked Rosie round.

Rhoda was still upstairs.

Mum said, "Rhoda went to confession last week."

Doreen shrugged.

"I think she's really sorry for what she did."

"I wish it would stop raining," said Doreen. "Then I could get away from certain people."

Doreen's wish was granted. The rain eased on Monday, and for the next week or so it was fine enough between showers to stretch a skipping rope across the street or go to the woods with Barbara and June and, sometimes, Rosie.

Rhoda didn't come. Doreen had rejected all her overtures of friendship and Rhoda seemed at last to have taken the hint. She stayed at home and cooked, or did things to her hair, or went to Aunty Elsie's.

Doreen's gang – she thought of it as her gang, although June was a rival leader – roamed the woods, playing P.P. or A.R.A.; all their games were known by initials, like the Services and the programmes on the wireless.

There were other gangs in the woods. The boys were mostly involved in battles: Brummie evacuees versus Scousers, with the locals divided between them; or Scousers and Brummies in a brief alliance waging war on the locals. The boys swung from trees, stalked each other, laid ambushes, but few of the battles were ferocious.

The girls didn't go in for battles, but they had their own ways of making war. June got fed up with Rosie and tried to make her go home, but Doreen always became protective if anyone else bullied Rosie. "Leave her alone," she said. "She can come if she likes." And Barbara backed her up.

"She's dim and she's snotty," said June when Rosie was out of earshot.

"I know," said Doreen, "but she can't help it."

She felt a responsibility for Rosie because she lived next door and they had known each other all their lives.

June fell out with Doreen and attached herself to a group of tough girls led by Joyce Revell. Doreen was afraid of them. Joyce's gang took to following Doreen's and yelling abuse or charging in and breaking up their games.

There was a constant struggle among the Culverton children for use of the Dungeon. It was the best place in Old Works. The boys often took it over, but sometimes Joyce's gang drove them off. If Doreen and her friends got there first, Joyce's gang would come up the back way onto the broken roof and shout insults and shower them with twigs and pine cones.

Graffiti appeared on the wall of the Dungeon:

"D.D. IS STUCK UP."

"DOREEN L. SNOT-FACE."

It was a shock, seeing her own name. Doreen felt humiliated, even a bit scared. She remembered a rhyme Dad used to say:

Sticks and stones may break my bones
But words can never hurt me.

It wasn't true. Words were the worst.

She pretended not to care. "Stupid nits."

"What does it say?" asked Rosie. She couldn't read much.

"Nothing," Barbara said quickly.

"They needn't think we're scared," said Doreen.

But they were. Lennie told Doreen about a ruined cottage in the woods off Love Lane; they'd try going there, Doreen thought.

In the end there was no need to move. A scheme was organized to get children onto neighbouring farms to help with the harvest, but you had to be twelve or over. So Rhoda went, and Joyce Revell, and most of her friends; June was left without a gang and tried to get back into Doreen's but they drove her off.

Suddenly the weather worsened. There were thunderstorms day after day, and rain that could soak you in seconds. The harvest was abandoned; the woods emptied of children. Doreen read *The Call of the Wild* and then started on *Little Women*. Rhoda went to Aunty Elsie's to help with the costumes.

Like the weather, Rhoda changed. She seemed nervous and edgy – "funny", as Doreen put it.

"It's the thunder," said Mum. "Gives you headaches."

But it wasn't that.

On the Saturday before they went back to school Phyl came round with her baby, Ian. She often came when Mum was off work, and would sit and drink tea and complain about living with her mother-in-law.

Doreen and Rhoda put aside their differences for a while and played with Ian. He was not quite walking, and they encouraged him to stagger between them as they knelt on the hearth-rug with outstretched arms.

Phyl was deep in conversation with Mum. Doreen half-listened, as she always did when grown-ups were talking. "And another thing, Mum, she goes on at me if I want to go out of an evening. I'd like to go out with my friends from work – I miss work – but she thinks I should just stay in every night and write to Jim."

"Well, you'll come to our concert, won't you, next Saturday? See your old mum making a fool of herself?"

"You'll be the best, Mum!" insisted Phyl. "And don't worry, I won't let her stop me coming to that." She turned to the two girls on the hearth-rug. "You're in it, too, aren't you,

Rhoda? I saw the poster."

Doreen's head jerked up. Rhoda, in the concert? *Rhoda?* She couldn't be. No children, Miss Forrest had said...

She looked at Rhoda and saw that her face had flooded with scarlet.

So it was true.

"Poster?" Rhoda stammered. "Where?" She wouldn't meet Doreen's eye.

Doreen sprang to her feet, fists clenched. She looked at her mother. Had she known? But she could see from her face that she hadn't.

Ian began to cry. Phyl soothed him, unaware of the effect her remark had had. "They must have just gone up," she said. "I saw one in the High Street, in Jennings' window, when I got off the bus. All those names. There's a lot of people in it..."

"Doreen – " began Rhoda.

"I'm going out," said Doreen.

She ran all the way to the High Street, and stopped outside Jennings'. There it was: a proper printed poster, with a drawing at the top of someone playing a piano, and underneath the list of performers: "Miss Hilda West ... Mrs Elsie Meadows ... Mrs Adeline Dyer..." and, last of all, "Miss Rhoda Kelly".

CHAPTER NINE

"Doreen!"

Rhoda was running down the street towards her. She arrived panting. "Doreen – don't think – I'm not going to do it unless you can – "

"Yes, you are!" said Doreen. "It says here you are: 'Miss Rhoda Kelly'. No mention of me." She was burning up with anger. She had wanted so much to be in the concert; the thought of Rhoda being in it and not her was unbearable. "Now I know what you've been doing up at Aunty Elsie's! Getting round Miss Forrest – "

"I meant to tell you – "

"You didn't! You never meant to tell me anything!"

"It was only last week. I went to Aunty Elsie's and Miss Forrest was there."

"So you showed off and sang for her."

"She was interested... Doreen, I *asked* her

if you could do it too. She was interested because of my mother – "

"Oh, yes, of course, your wonderful mother, who's so famous and beautiful. Only we've never seen her. Maybe she doesn't exist, like your boyfriend. Like your father – "

"He does!"

Doreen saw that she had touched a nerve and continued relentlessly. "She might as well not exist. She never writes. She never visits. You don't even know where she lives. She doesn't care much about you, does she? She doesn't want you and neither do we."

"Your mam does. She likes me."

"No, she doesn't. She's just being polite. She thinks you're precocious; she told me so. The only thing my mum likes about you is the ten and six a week."

Rhoda was silent. "I hate you," she said at last. And she turned away and began to walk back towards home.

Doreen felt a flicker of guilt; she'd gone too far. "Well, it's true, isn't it?" she shouted after Rhoda. "You *don't* know your mother's address!"

After Rhoda had gone, Doreen stayed in the High Street. She was shaking. She walked up and down, looking in shop windows, seeing over and over again the offending poster and letting it reinforce her anger and convince her that she had been entitled to say what she had.

When she got home there was no sign of Rhoda. Phyl and Ian had gone and Mum was ironing.

"*There* you are," said Mum. She looked wary, as if Doreen were an unexploded bomb.

"Where's Rhoda?" asked Doreen.

"Upstairs. She was very quiet when she came in. Went straight up. Have you two sorted it all out?"

"Oh, yes, it's all sorted out – she's in the concert and I'm not."

"That's not what I meant. Has she explained? She told me and Phyl that she'd asked Miss Forrest if you could be in it, too. She says she doesn't want to do it otherwise."

"She's got herself on the poster, though, hasn't she?"

Mum sighed, and thumped the iron down. "Poor Phyl – she wondered what she'd said. Listen, can you three get your own tea tonight? I've told Rhoda. I'm going to Aunty Elsie's; she's made me a dress and it needs fitting. There's a vegetable pie in the larder—"

"If that's the one Rhoda made I don't want it."

"Doreen! I know you're angry with Rhoda. But you'll eat that pie."

Doreen smouldered. "All right."

There was silence from upstairs. Doreen didn't want to face Rhoda, so she went into the front room and found *Little Women* and lay on the floor and read.

After a while Mum put her head round the door and said, "I'm off, then. Now, don't brood. It'll all sort itself out. I'll have a word with Elsie. Don't forget the blackout curtains."

"I won't."

There was still no sound from Rhoda.

Lennie came home at five fifteen. "Where's Mum?"

"Aunty Elsie's. We're to get our own tea."

She got up and began laying the table. The vegetable pie looked good. Rhoda had made it from a recipe in *Woman's Weekly*.

"Rhoda!" Lennie called.

"Leave her," said Doreen, but Lennie was halfway up the stairs, calling again. She heard a muffled voice: "... not hungry."

"What's up with her?" Lennie asked.

"We had a row." Doreen explained, giving her own side of the story with much feeling, but Lennie was unmoved.

"Girls!" he said dismissively, and cut a slice of pie.

Lennie was going to the pictures with some friends. After he had gone, Doreen cleared away and washed up noisily, venting her anger on the plates and hoping Rhoda could hear. Then she went into the front room and curled up on the settee with her book.

After a while she became aware of sounds overhead: footsteps back and forth, drawers opening and shutting. Then she heard Rhoda come downstairs and go out of the back door and down the passage.

She sprang to her feet and looked out. Rhoda had turned left and was walking rapidly away. Doreen saw her red curls bouncing above the level of the Lloyds' privet hedge.

She put *Little Women* down and went upstairs.

Rhoda's things were gone: the photograph of her mother, the holy picture with its glints of gold, the rosary, the combs and hair slides and mascara. Her Bible and her dressing-gown were gone from the chair beside the bed.

Doreen knew what she would find but she checked anyway. She pulled back the curtain of the makeshift wardrobe: Rhoda's spare dress and cardigan were missing. The dressing-table drawers were empty. The nightdress was gone from under her pillow.

The full implication didn't strike Doreen at first. She thought, Idiot; she's gone to Aunty Elsie's to tell tales. Then she remembered that Rhoda had turned left out of the front gate. If she'd been going to Aunty Elsie's she would have turned right.

She was going to the railway station – to catch a train home to Liverpool.

Doreen felt alarm flood through her. Mum would be frantic. She'd want to know what Doreen had said to Rhoda. And Doreen didn't want to tell her. But if Mum went after Rhoda, or got the police or whatever people did, and Rhoda was brought home, *she'd* tell.

I have to get her back, Doreen thought, even if it means saying sorry. She ran downstairs.

The clock on the kitchen mantelpiece said seven-forty-five. Doreen didn't know the times of the trains. She tried to remember if she'd heard one go by since Rhoda left, but couldn't think; you got so used to the sound.

It was raining outside. The evening had closed in early, heavy clouds massing without a break. Doreen put on her mac and ran out of the house.

The station was deserted, except for a porter sweeping the far end of the platform. No sign of Rhoda. Doreen checked the waiting-room and the ladies'. She was too late; the train must have gone.

The porter was calling to her. He came closer.

"No trains going west, love. Not till tomorrow. Derailment up the line."

"Tomorrow?"

"Five-forty-five in the morning, the first one."

"Did you see a girl? Red hair and a blue raincoat?"

"Yes. I told her the same."

Thank goodness, Doreen thought. "Where did she go?"

He shrugged and tilted his head the way Doreen had come. "Home, I suppose."

Home. Of course. She'd be home by now. Odd that they hadn't passed each other. But perhaps she had gone along the lane and in through the back gate to avoid the embarrassment of being seen. That must be it.

Doreen raced home.

But Rhoda wasn't there, and there was no sign that she had been back. Doreen checked everywhere, even the pigeon loft and the coal store. Perhaps she *had* gone to Aunty Elsie's. And yet it wasn't likely. Mum had told Rhoda that she was going there herself, and Rhoda wouldn't want to face Mum, not after the things Doreen had said...

Doreen felt guilty. She knew she should never have said what she had about Mum. It wasn't true about the ten and six, and as for the other – well, it had been said in confidence, and to cheer Doreen up; she shouldn't have repeated it.

She remembered the graffiti at the Dungeon, and how she'd felt.

"Is it true? Is it kind? Is it necessary?" The things she'd said to Rhoda were none of those. She didn't want Rhoda to go away to Liverpool thinking that she'd meant them.

Where could Rhoda have gone? She wasn't friendly enough with Barbara to have gone to the Lees'. Miss Wingfield, perhaps? But Miss Wingfield lived out at Cray's Common, five miles away. Perhaps she had a telephone? If she did Rhoda might know the number and have gone to phone her.

There was a telephone box in the High Street. It was worth a try. She ran all the way there.

The High Street was empty. The shops were shut; only the pubs were open. Rhoda wouldn't go into a pub. If she *had* phoned Miss Wingfield for a lift she would still have been waiting by the phone box.

Doreen walked home, thinking. Rhoda knew the next train was due early in the morning. If she was determined to catch it she would want to wait somewhere nearby – somewhere sheltered, where no one would think of looking for her.

Doreen put herself in Rhoda's place; she imagined leaving the station, not wanting to go home or tell anyone what she was doing, looking for somewhere to hide.

Old Works.

Old Works was less than ten minutes' walk from the station; and the Dungeon, where its roof was still intact, was dry.

And by the time I get there, Doreen thought, it'll be dark as well.

CHAPTER TEN

The house was in darkness. Doreen went from room to room, putting up the blackout. She had to drag chairs about and stand on them to reach, but at last every room was done and she could switch on a light.

She felt lonely, and scared, and wished Lennie hadn't gone out; he might have agreed to go with her to Old Works.

When the lights were off, the street outside had still held a glimmer of daylight, but now, when she peeped out from within the lighted house, the sky looked black.

The thought of going out alone filled her with fear. And would Rhoda be at Old Works? Would she really have gone there, knowing she'd have to stay all night in the pitch dark?

I couldn't, Doreen thought.

But Rhoda was different. Doreen remembered that evening at Old Works with Lennie.

Rhoda hadn't been frightened by the gathering dusk. And besides, where else could she have gone?

I'll go quickly, Doreen thought. I don't have to go into the Dungeon. I'll call. I'll tell her I'm sorry and we'll be back home before Mum finds out...

She switched off the light and opened the back door. Rain was falling in a steady soft drizzle. She took her mac from its peg and went outside.

The street was black, no street lamps, not a chink of light showing from any of the blacked-out houses.

Doreen never went out in the blackout on her own. None of her friends did. They were always home before dark; it was like a curfew. Trips to the the cinema or to Aunty Elsie's with Mum or Lennie were different. Then the darkness was exciting: full of chatter and the rustle and scent of chips wrapped in newspaper. Now she was conscious only of the *tap-tap* of her footsteps on the pavement.

Farther on, in the lane that led between hedges to Old Works, the shadows deepened and she couldn't see where she was putting her feet and there was nothing ahead but the dark and the patter of rain on leaves. She felt utterly alone.

I won't know when I'm there, she thought. But somehow she did; her feet took her the familiar way, in among the ruined buildings, past the entrance to the tunnel. Her eyes gradually made out the outlines of walls and tree-stumps. The works went into a hollow, and down there was the entrance to the Dungeon.

The hollow was a cup of darkness.

I'll call, she thought.

Her voice was thin in the empty space. "Rhoda! Are you there? Rhoda!"

No reply.

An owl hooted. Even in bed at night the sound of owls frightened Doreen.

"Rhoda!" Her voice rose, panicky, on the last syllable. "Rhoda, I'm scared! Please come out!"

She began to tremble. Perhaps Rhoda couldn't hear her because of the rain. Or didn't want to. Perhaps she wasn't there at all, and Doreen was alone in Old Works.

The wavering cry came again.

"It's just an owl," she said angrily, aloud. The rain fell harder. Its roar surrounded her. Her hair was streaming wet and water was running down her neck, and she dared not go into the hollow.

She remembered another way. An easier way in the dark. There was a well-beaten path through the woods onto the roof of the Dungeon; all the children used it. You could walk onto the roof, and where it was broken you could look down into the room below.

She felt for the path. Brambles caught her legs, and once she tripped on a tree root and nearly fell. She stopped then, and shouted, but there was no answer. She became almost convinced that she was wrong, that Rhoda wasn't there at all, but at Aunty Elsie's, telling everything, and being given cocoa and a bed for the night...

She reached the roof. The ground felt different, harder, underfoot, and led up in a slight curve. Now she had to be careful. She squatted and felt wet brickwork beneath her hand.

She called again.

Still no answer. But did she hear something – a rustling – or was it some animal? The hiss of rain blurred other sounds.

Something moved below, she was sure.

"Rhoda! It's Doreen!"

She inched forward on hands and knees. There was a tree, a rowan, growing between the bricks near the drop. She reached out and found it, held on, and felt for the edge of the broken roof with her free hand.

"Rhoda!"

That movement again, and then she saw it: the pale oval of a face.

"Go away," said Rhoda.

A great wave of relief washed over Doreen.

"I can't," she said. "You've got to come home. Mum will be so worried." She found that her teeth were chattering. "Please, Rhoda.

I'm sorry I said those things. They weren't true." She leaned forward, trying to see some response in the upturned face. "I never meant to – "

And suddenly the bricks moved under her hand; she lurched, seized at the tree to save herself and swung out over the drop as the roof gave way and bricks and earth showered down. She heard screaming – her own and Rhoda's mixed – and then the branch snapped and she fell, landing hard on the rubble. She hid her face from the rush of earth and stones. The battering on her back continued, slowed, and at last stopped.

For a while she lay stunned. Then, cautiously, she raised herself onto her knees. She hurt all over and she could feel blood trickling into one eye.

"Rhoda?" she whispered. "Are you all right?"

But there was no answer.

Rhoda was somewhere beneath her, buried under the rubble.

CHAPTER ELEVEN

Doreen moved fast. She sprang off the mound of rubble, and began to pull away bricks and stones, heaving them to one side. She sobbed as she worked, "It's all right, Rhoda. Don't worry. It'll be all right."

There was no response. She began to panic as she scraped and scrabbled and brushed away earth. She touched cloth – Rhoda's raincoat; her shoulder; her hair. If only she could see! Rhoda was so still and silent. Doreen found her face and brushed earth from her nose and mouth.

"Rhoda!" she begged. "Wake up! Please wake up! Don't die!"

There was no movement.

A picture came into her mind – not something she'd seen but something she'd been told – of women gathered at a pit head, and a miner brought out, dead, with scarcely a mark on him, suffocated by the fall of earth and stone when the roof collapsed.

Suffocated. Rhoda was suffocated.

She sprang up in terror and ran outside.

She had to get help.

Despite her panic, a part of her brain was thinking fast. There must be a telephone at the station, but it would take ten minutes to get there, probably more in the dark. Much nearer was the Revells'; their smallholding was just up the lane.

But first she had to find her way out of the hollow.

She found the place where the path led up, and began to climb, scrambling up the muddy slope on hands and knees, grabbing at tussocks and brambles, not caring about the pain.

She reached the top, picked her way across the dangerous area of ruined walls, and then began to run. The path was just visible between darker masses of trees, and she ran uncaring of where she put her feet. Her fear of the dark was gone too; all that mattered now was to see houses and people – most of all, people.

There was a short cut to the Revells' that Joyce always took: a smaller path leading off to the left. It brought you out almost opposite the smallholding. Somehow Doreen found it. She raced along, feeling nettles whip her legs, thinking only that Rhoda was dead, that she must tell someone, she must get help.

She came out on the road, crossed it, found the drive that led to the smallholding. She saw the dark shape of buildings against the sky. "Help!" she shouted. "Help, please!"

A dog began to bark, then another; and far away, towards Station Road, a third dog added its voice. She heard people, and saw light – light at last, and such a bright one! A hurricane lamp was bobbing towards her, and a woman's voice, with a nervous edge to it, called, "Who's that?"

"Doreen! Doreen Dyer! I need help!"

She reached the woman. It was Molly, Joyce's sister. The hurricane lamp made a great blaze of light between them. Doreen stretched a hand towards it. "The blackout..." she whispered.

"Bugger the blackout," said Molly. "What's up?"

"She's dead," said Doreen. "I killed her."

Her teeth chattered as she spoke. She hadn't stopped shaking since Mrs Revell brought her home.

Lennie tried to reassure her. "She might not be. She might just have been unconscious."

"Lennie, you didn't see what happened. All the earth... It all fell on her. And the bricks. And me on top. She couldn't breathe."

"But you got all the stuff off her. You were

quick. They get roof falls all the time in mines, and people survive."

"*Do* they?"

"Of course. Here, drink your tea." He handed her the cup. If Doreen hadn't been in such a state she would have laughed: Lennie making *her* tea! But Mum had told him to, before she went off with Mrs Revell.

Doreen sat in Dad's chair now, wearing her nightie and socks, with a blanket wrapped around her. While she sipped her tea, Lennie told her stories of men who'd been rescued in mining accidents. Slowly her shaking subsided.

At half past ten Lennie said, "I'd best make the fire up. Mum'll be cold when she gets back."

The hospital was at Wraybury. "How long does it take to get there?" Doreen asked.

"Not long in an ambulance. Twenty minutes?"

"They've been gone hours. Lennie, how will Mum get home?"

"I don't know. Perhaps someone will bring her."

"If only she could get a message to us!" She began to cry. "It was all my fault."

"Don't be daft," said Lennie. "That roof could have gone at any time. The rain we've been having – that would have weakened it, like. That and the kids climbing on it."

"I didn't mean the roof. I meant Rhoda going off there. Because of the things I said."

"What things?"

"I can't tell you. Horrible things."

"They can't have been that bad."

"They made her want to go home." Doreen was choking on her tears.

Lennie rearranged the blanket and hugged her awkwardly. "Look, Mum said you're not to get upset." He went to pick up the kettle. "I'll make some more tea."

All night they listened to the slow tick of the clock. Eleven o'clock came; twelve; twelve-thirty. Still no message, and no way of finding out what was happening.

"You'd better go to bed," said Lennie.

He made her a hot-water bottle.

"I'm not cold, it's nerves," said Doreen. But it was nice, all the same, to feel cared for.

She lay awake for a long time, reliving the events of the evening all jumbled up: the rush of earth, the screams, the awful stillness of Rhoda's body were mixed with the bumpy, rattling trip home in the Revells' cart and seeing the rain falling in the circle of light from the hurricane lamp.

She must have slept at last. The next thing she was aware of was the room full of daylight and Mum silhouetted against the window as she lifted down the blackout screen.

"Mum...?" The events of the night rushed

back to her, and she sat up, becoming aware of pulled muscles and bruises that she hadn't noticed before.

Mum turned round. "She's alive."

Doreen felt as if a weight as heavy as the brick roof had been lifted off her. She began to cry in relief. "I thought she was dead."

Mum hugged her – cautiously because of the bruises. "She might have been if you hadn't dug her out so quickly. She came round in the ambulance. She's got a broken collar bone, badly bruised ribs, a lot of cuts and bruises."

"Where is she?"

"Still at the hospital. They kept her in overnight. Miss Wingfield will fetch her this afternoon."

"Good." She sank back on the pillows. But other anxieties began to surface. Her heart beat fast. "Did Rhoda talk ... much? Did she say why she went to the Dungeon?"

"She tried to explain, but I said we'd sort all that out later." She looked suspiciously at Doreen. "She was running away, wasn't she, because you'd quarrelled?"

Doreen fiddled with a loose thread on her eiderdown. "I didn't mean the things I said." She looked up, anxious. "She will stay, won't she? She won't have to be moved?"

"Do you want her to stay?"

Doreen looked around the room: at the empty chair where Rhoda's clothes had hung, the dressing-table swept clear of her possessions. It would seem odd, now, without Rhoda. But did she want her to stay? Or did she just want not to have made her go?

"Rhoda says it's all her fault," said Mum. "She says she should never have agreed to be in the concert without you."

Doreen thought about this. "The thing is, I think I would have done the same, if I'd had the chance."

"That's what I told her," said Mum.

"I'm sorry," Doreen said.

It was easier to say than she had expected. Rhoda looked such a victim: her right arm in a sling, and a great purple bruise on one cheekbone.

Not that Doreen had escaped unhurt. She had cuts to her face, but the worst thing was the bruised ribs. Mum had even thought of taking her to the doctor, but the expense put her off. "We'll see how you go," she said. "There's one thing: neither of you will be fit to sing in that concert now."

While Mum and Miss Wingfield were there, talking, Doreen and Rhoda had exclaimed at each other's appearance and compared injuries, pushing up sleeves and rolling down socks, and anticipating how much they would enjoy being celebrities around the town.

But now Miss Wingfield had left and

Mum had gone upstairs, leaving them alone.

"I'm sorry, too," said Rhoda.

Doreen glanced at Rhoda's brown paper carrier bag, soggy and disintegrating in the corner where Miss Wingfield had dumped it. Nothing had been unpacked.

"Will you stay here now?"

"Do you want me to?"

But before Doreen could answer, the back door opened and Lennie burst in.

"Rhoda! *Your mother's here!*"

CHAPTER TWELVE

"They're in a car," said Lennie. "Her and a soldier. I told them to come in."

He went to the foot of the stairs and called, "Mum!"

And then they heard voices, and the click of high-heeled shoes, and Anne-Marie came into the room.

Red-gold hair, blue eyes that flicked around. She was like Rhoda, Doreen thought; like her own photograph, too, and yet different – harder. She wore a tight-fitting dark blue costume and held a lighted cigarette in her hand.

"Mam!" Tears ran down Rhoda's face. She rose awkwardly to her feet and tried to hug her mother.

Anne-Marie fended her off. "Easy, love, you'll get ash on my skirt." She waved the cigarette distractedly, looking for an ashtray. Doreen found her a saucer and she stubbed it out. "Thanks."

As Mum came downstairs and into the room, Anne-Marie was holding Rhoda at arms' length and exclaiming, "You look awful! What have you been doing to yourself?"

Mum took in the situation and began to explain, but Anne-Marie interrupted. "Oh, I know. Some woman phoned me – Miss Winford? Said there'd been an accident and I ought to come straightaway. You can imagine the shock – I was due back on stage in fifteen minutes. I told her, 'I can't just drop everything like that; I've got my public to consider.' But she laid it on about Rhoda needing me – " she glanced at her daughter as if expecting her to deny this – "and then after the show Harry said, 'You'd better go; I'll take you tomorrow.'"

She introduced the soldier, who was standing by the door holding a bouquet of flowers and a brown paper carrier bag. "This is Sergeant Wilson; supposed to be on leave, poor man – " she smiled and squeezed his arm – "but he's driven me all the way from Bootle." She turned to Rhoda again. "Those bruises look terrible; I've got some foundation that might hide them."

"I expect you'd like a cup of tea," said Mum. She smiled at the sergeant and indicated Dad's chair. "Do sit down."

"We'd love one!" exclaimed Anne-Marie.

"Parched, aren't we, Harry? We've been on the road for hours, Mrs..."

"Dyer," said Mum. "I wrote to you."

"Oh, yes, you did. Ta. I'd been meaning to get in touch."

She took the flowers from Sergeant Wilson. "These are for you, Mrs Dyer. And some chocolates in the carrier."

The three children swooped on the carrier bag while Mum took the flowers.

Anne-Marie perched on one of the kitchen chairs, twitching her narrow skirt down over her knees. "Now, tell me, love," she said to Rhoda, "are you really all right?" And then, before Rhoda could answer, she turned back to Mum. "The woman who rang said not to worry, but you can't help it, can you? Not that I couldn't have done with a lie-in today; I'm dead tired."

She lit a cigarette and offered the packet to Mum, who shook her head. She inhaled, and leaned back, gazing critically at Rhoda as she blew out smoke. "What have you done to your hair? It looks a mess."

"She got earth in it," Doreen said coldly. "When the roof fell in." She put her arm around Rhoda.

"Needs cutting," said Anne-Marie. "I can see the split ends from here."

Doreen noticed Mum's lips tightening. She doesn't like her, she thought; and neither do I.

Anne-Marie was rummaging in her handbag. "Before I forget, there's a letter for you, Rhoda." She tossed her an envelope. "From Bernadette. I promised I'd send it and I've been carrying it round for weeks."

Rhoda grabbed the letter eagerly and put it in her cardigan pocket unopened.

"I don't know what the woman finds to write about," laughed Anne-Marie. "She never goes anywhere. My dressmaker," she explained to Mum. "Keeps an eye on Rhoda sometimes."

Doreen thought the letter looked fat and interesting.

Mum got up and poured the tea. Doreen noticed how her eyes kept straying to the flowers. They were beautiful: bronze and crimson and gold chrysanthemums mixed with some big white daisies, and greenery spread around at the back.

"Could you put them in water, Doreen? There's your nan's vase in the front room. We could all sit in the front room," she added, opening the door, but nobody moved. The sergeant was comfortable in Dad's chair, and Anne-Marie said, "Oh, don't bother, Mrs Dyer. We can't stay. We just popped in to make sure the kid's still in one piece."

Rhoda helped Doreen with the flowers. She showed her how to cut the stems diagonally and take off the lower leaves and arrange everything in the vase.

"Mum's never had flowers before – not shop ones," said Doreen.

"Me mam gets given them all the time."

And Doreen realized, then, that the bouquet must be one that Anne-Marie had been given last night, after the performance.

Lennie was talking to the sergeant, and Mum was trying to explain to Anne-Marie how Rhoda came to be injured. Doreen listened, hoping Mum wouldn't say they'd quarrelled. But Mum was tactful and spoke of "some game they got up to – although I've told Doreen often enough not to go there."

"These things happen," said Anne-Marie. Her laugh rang out. "You send your kid away from the bombing and she still gets buried under a pile of bricks."

Mum had already brought out some biscuits. She offered sandwiches.

"No, no. We ate on the way here," the sergeant assured her.

"We could open the chocolates," suggested Doreen.

So they drank tea and ate chocolates, and the pile of lipstick-stained cigarette stubs grew in the saucer, and Anne-Marie talked about the shows she'd been in and the bombing they'd had, and Lennie took the sergeant out to the loft to look at the pigeons, and Mum remembered to get Anne-Marie to write down her address.

"Although I'll be moving again soon." She turned to Rhoda. "I'll send you a card, love. I'm going to Aberystwyth for a month or so."

Rhoda's face brightened. "There wouldn't be any bombing in Aberystwyth. I could visit you."

"Oh, love, it's not worth it. My lodgings are tiny – you've no idea, Mrs Dyer, how much easier it is to get lodgings when you haven't got a kid with you. You'd be bored to death, Rhoda. And besides, I'll be back in Merseyside before Christmas. You're better off staying put. She's no trouble, is she, Mrs Dyer? People always tell me she's no trouble."

"Of course not," said Mum with feeling. "She's a lovely girl. You should be proud of her."

Lennie and Sergeant Wilson came in. The sergeant glanced at the clock on the mantelpiece. "Well, Annie?"

Anne-Marie got up. "Yes, we must be on our way." She glanced in the mirror and touched her hair.

"Coming for a little drive" the sergeant asked Rhoda, "before you say goodbye?"

"Oh, yes!" Rhoda followed them out. Doreen would have gone too, but Mum held her back. "Let Rhoda be with her mother."

The kitchen looked as if they'd had a party, littered with tea cups and chocolate wrappers and cigarette stubs. Draped over a chair was a black velvet jacket that Anne-Marie had brought for Rhoda.

"Well!" said Mum.

Doreen exploded: "She doesn't care about Rhoda! Mum, she just doesn't *care*!"

Mum put her arms round her. "Don't get upset, Doreen. There's nothing you can do about it."

Doreen hid her face in Mum's cardigan. "But she's awful," she said.

Lennie took three pound notes out of his pocket and gave them to Mum. "From the sergeant – towards Rhoda's keep. He said, 'Annie won't think.'"

Mum sighed. "No more she did! And I couldn't get a word in to ask her. Never mind! Open the window, Lennie – the room's full of smoke and scent. We'll have Aunty Elsie here any minute, come to see how you girls are; I sent a message. And, Doreen, she's bringing frocks to try on. She's made two out of some fire-damaged stuff she got at the market: one for each of you. They'll do for school."

School started on Wednesday, Doreen remembered. "We won't go to the same school," she said, "me and Rhoda."

"Those Catholic school kids get picked on," said Lennie.

"She'll be all right. I'll stick up for her."

Mum lifted Rhoda's bag. "I'll take this

up – " she turned to Doreen – "shall I?"

"Yes. And we could move that screen. We won't want it now."

Doreen and Rhoda went to bed early, on Mum's orders.

Rhoda's Bible and rosary and pictures were back in their places. Doreen looked at the photograph of Anne-Marie.

I like her better as a photograph, she thought. Perhaps Rhoda does, too.

Rhoda was holding her hairbrush awkwardly in her left hand. "I can't brush my hair."

"I'll do it," said Doreen. She took the brush. "Miss Kelly, I know there's a shortage of shampoo, but did you have to wash your hair in mud?"

"You're daft," Rhoda said; there was a smile in her voice. Still with her back to Doreen, she asked, "It's all right, then, is it? You want me to stay?"

"Yes," said Doreen.

"Till the war's over?"

"Yes."

"It might be months."

They laughed, and Doreen said, "It might be years."